Bet They'll MISS US WHEN We're Gone

D0026883

MARIANNE WIGGINS

HarperPerennial
A Division of HarperCollinsPublishers

"Angel" first appeared in *Bomb*; "Millions" in *Harper's*; "A Cup of Jo" in *The Paris Review*; and "Croeso I Gymru" under the title "Internal Exile" in *The Los Angeles Times Magazine*; "Grocer's Daughter" is reprinted with permission from *Parade*, © 1990.

A hardcover edition of this book was published in 1991 by HarperCollins Publishers.

HarperCollins books may be purchased for educational, business, or sales promotional use. For information, please call or write: Special Markets Department, HarperCollins Publishers, Inc., 10 East 53rd Street, New York, NY 10022. Telephone: (212) 207-7528; Fax: (212) 207-7222.

First HarperPerennial edition published 1992.

Designed by Karen Savary

The Library of Congress has catalogued the hardcover edition as follows:

Wiggins, Marianne.
    Bet they'll miss us when we're gone : stories / Marianne Wiggins.
    —1st ed.
      p. cm.
    ISBN 0-06-016139-6
    I. Title.
PS3573.I385B48   1991   89-46130
    813'.54—dc20

ISBN 0-06-092164-1 (pbk.)

92 93 94 95 96 AC/MB 10 9 8 7 6 5 4 3 2 1

ALSO BY MARIANNE WIGGINS

Babe
Went South
Separate Checks
Herself in Love
John Dollar

remembering my father

CONTENTS

I am grateful to
the National Endowment for the Arts
and
the Mrs. Giles Whiting Foundation.

—M.W.

Bet They'll
MISS US WHEN
We're Gone

ANGEL

GOD LIVED ON THE WICK inside the glass of oil and water on top of the old woman's chest of drawers where He was kept alive as if He were a lightning bug inside a jar. God lived in other places too, places much more natural to Him, places He belonged, like funeral parlors and adoption homes, where there were people trained to talk to Him, who could look after Him as He got old, the young girl knew. He did not belong on Ya-yia's chest of drawers. He did not belong inside a glass. He did not belong in circles on the ceiling in the dark where the young girl slept along the wall beside the kitchen after her parents drove away and left her in the hottest place in all Virginia with the old Greek woman, Fanny.

She could count the words that she and Fanny had in common. There were forty. Some were Greek and some were English. Some were words like *yardthi*, *roofi*, *striti*. Some were counting words like *ena*, *thia*, *tria*, *pente*, *ex*. Fanny never spoke the English or the Greek for number four. She acted like the number wasn't there. She never used or said it, which was strange, because she had four sons. And another thing about her was that she had diabetes. These two facts were not connected except in the girl's mind as she counted slowly when she filled Fanny's syringe. Some other words they spoke to one another were *hypo, insulin, come help, what time is it?, teevee.* All the other words were names: Papou (Fanny's husband, dead); Maria (Fanny's daughter); Michee, Nichee, Archie, Yorgi (Fanny's four sons); and the Dots.

The Dots were the girl's aunts, the wives of Fanny's sons. There were four of them and none of them were Greek. Michee—that was Fanny's word for Uncle Mike—married a woman called Dot when he came back from the navy and she was skinny and she came from Danville and she wore a diamond in her crucifix and she crossed herself from left to right, the wrong way, in the *ekklesia*, and Fanny learned to speak her name as if it formed a category the day Nichee brought a woman home from North Carolina. Nichee's other name was Uncle Nick and Nichee's Dot worked at the percale factory and had a trophy in her house from when she'd won Miss Conviviality. Her real name was Cat. She was the size of several Miss Convivialities now and had a mustache stained from nicotine and she wore dresses made from imperfect sheets that she got free from the percale factory. Since the girl had known her the labels on the outside of Cat's dresses had progressed from TWIN to STANDARD to FULL SIZE. Known collectively, like sirens, the Dots were never singularly named, but the other two were Brenda and Jeanette, and Fanny never spoke to them because none of them, not even one among the four, had done her bit and had a child. Brenda, who wore pedal pushers and bolero tops that showed her midriff and whose favorite lipstick was called Red on Red, told the girl the whole truth one afternoon when they were sitting on a blanket in the backyard about how all four of Fanny's boys had got the mumps at the same time one summer when they all were just beginning to get manly.

Ignorance and immigrants go gland in hand, she said, and the girl had known that she was hearing higher wisdom from a higher source, even though she didn't understand it, because then Brenda said, "You'll see, Angel. You keep finding out most things too late in life." Then Brenda said what she wanted was a sugar baby even if it had to come from some passing stranger for a daddy but, she said, George wasn't on her side so she was takin' vitamins. She was takin' lots of exercise, she said, and laughed. Soon after that there was the trouble about George skipping bail when he had shot a passing stranger in the backyard running from the bedroom. Then Brenda cleared her stuff out of their house and gave her the collected tubes of Red on Red, which were a lot and only half-used because Brenda hated using lipsticks once they got all flatty on the top, she said. She gave the girl a pair of genuine white cotton gloves, mismatched, and some beads and two high-heeled shoes, also mismatched. Then George turned himself in to try to get Brenda to come back, but she never did and their house went into foreclosure and he went to jail and never looked the same. His hair went white which made his skin look yellow. The night before he went to jail he came to Fanny's house and took the girl and Fanny out to High's for ice cream. Fanny had vanilla like she always had, the girl had peach. George cried a lot and Fanny cried a little, then they shouted at each other a long while in Greek. The girl was used to so much shouting. Every Sunday morning since she'd lived there, Michee, Nichee, Arch and George came over to the house to eat and shout.

Sunday mornings Fanny and the girl woke and the girl gave Fanny her insulin then Fanny made sweet coffee in the brass *kafes* while the girl took up the household rugs. When it was raining, rugs were hung on the back porch and beaten by the two of them with willow rackets and when it wasn't raining, rugs were shaken on the lawn then laid out on the grass and hosed. This happened daily. While they dried,

Fanny, in her flannel dusting slippers, buffed the floor. But on Sundays Fanny let the girl take charge of all the rugs alone while she washed and oiled her hair. Her hair was longer than her self and she carried it in three loops on her arm when it was loose and it weighed more when it was wet than the two gray rugs from the kitchen put together. It wasn't white, more like a heavy liquid silver, like a river of bright mercury. The girl worked hard on Sunday mornings just to finish with the rugs in time to be inside the kitchen when Fanny came in in her nightslip carrying her hair to lay it out and oil it on the table. The girl believed the hair belonged to someone else before it had belonged to Fanny—she believed the hair had grown the woman, that the hair had history and a language that the woman didn't have and that the woman was the growth of many years with which it chose to decorate itself. This belief, like all the girl's beliefs, was fleeting because when the hair was oiled, Fanny coiled it, then, with some strategic pins stuck in, it disappeared. It became the back of Fanny's head. To the girl its transformation from a river to a knot was as magical a change as anything the Ghost could do, and it put her in the mood for church. In church she stared hard at the icons and wondered why the men saints—George and Mike and Andrew—showed their hair and why the Virgin didn't. In church the incense made her sick in summer and in winter incense and the dark-eyed saints made her feel outlandish, like an alien inside some foreign smoky borders. After church she and Fanny walked the twelve blocks home and Fanny put on an apron and dressed the lamb and put it in the oven while the girl squeezed lemons for the soup and then her uncles came and shouted. What they shouted she was never sure. She listened for a word she knew but words she knew were never used. She knew that *Panayia* meant the Virgin, she knew *scata* meant shit, because anybody, even children in a foreign place, she knew, can tell the holy words from all the others, and the curses. But what the reason for the shouting was she had to let herself imagine. She imagined something made the shouting necessary, part of what they had to do, as if there was no choice. She imagined it was so the dead could hear, and she imagined that the dead were shouting somewhere too and sometimes staring at the glass in which God lived she pretended she was dead and pressed her lips together in an imitation of death's mask and took a breath and made a shout with her whole being till she shook with the full violence of its silence, then she came alive again and thought about the things that might begin to happen on the day she took a breath that finally blew God's candle out.

After Yorgi went to jail the girl and Fanny went to visit him each Friday. Angel was not allowed to go inside until it was discovered Fanny couldn't read or speak so they sent a prison guard to go for her because they thought the girl would translate for them. For this purpose Angel taught her grandmother the word *okay*. The guard would say, Tell the old woman she can talk to him ten minutes, and Angel would turn to Fanny and point toward the prison clock and say the word for ten but not the word for minutes 'cause she didn't know it and then Fanny would nod her head and tell the guard *oké*. Then the guard would say to Angel, Tell her I need to search her purse, and Angel would say *pursi* and Fanny would nod and tell the guard *oké* and give the purse to Angel who would pass it over. Then the guard would root through all the stuff they'd brought for Yorgi (cigarettes, dolmathes, olives, halvah, toothpicks and dates) and then another guard would come and take Fanny away and Angel would sit down on the chair and kick her feet backwards and forwards as a way of passing time. I bet you'd like a Pepsi-Cola, this one guard said to her one day.

"No, thank you," Angel knew enough to answer.

7

"I bet you would."

"Not really."

"Ice cold and ever'thang."

"Not especially."

"You shy?"

"No."

"Oh you're *not*?"

" 'Bout what?"

"Talkin' to a stranger."

"No."

"What's your name?"

"Angel."

"Cause you act like one?"

"One what?"

"One angel."

"Hard to say, ain't never seen one."

"*Hasn't* you?"

"Has *you*?"

"Sure!"

"Where?"

"Every evening you can see a bunch of angels down around the river."

"Oh I ain't allowed down there."

"Girl like you? Don't they think you're old enough?"

"Guess not."

"How old are you?"

"Almost eleven."

"I bet you're still in school."

"Not much."

"How come?"

"I'm dumb."

"I don't believe it."

"I made them think I can't talk like a normal person, you know. I made them think I'm dumb." She clamped her lips together. She clamped her knees together, too.

"You're jokin'!"

"No."

"Well, why'd you do a thang like that?"

"Because I felt like it."

"But here you are—you're talkin'!"

"I feel like it."

"But what if someone finds out?"

"Like how?"

"By listenin'."

"No one 'spects a mute to answer."

"You ain't worried?"

"About what?"

"Somebody turns you in?"

"Who'd do a thang like that?"

"*I* might."

"I doubt it."

"I'm kinda with the law in this capacity. I kinda have a duty."

"They'd never put a person of my age in jail," she said, but just in case, she put her hand around the empty hypo in the pocket of her pants and tried the sharpness of its needle with her fingernail.

"They could send you to a Home," the guard was saying just to scare her.

Angel smiled.

"How would you like that?" he asked. "Send you to a Home, nice pretty little thang like you?"

"I guess I'd hate it," Angel said.

"You bet!"

"I guess I'd suffer so's I'd start to try to find a way to kill myself."

"So there you are. You ought to try and start to act what you was named for."

Angel blinked and touched the needle. She thought the guard was saying something with a reference to her parents.

But then he just went on and on and talked to her about the things he'd seen, the ghosts down by the river.

Maybe Fanny had told Angel George's hair had turned white and Angel hadn't understood, but the first clue Angel had that George had changed was on that Sunday when Arch cried. It was too terrible. Arch was the second youngest of the four and last among them in the smarts department. All he'd ever wanted out of life was to paint exteriors but he'd fallen off a ladder through the windshield of a parked DeSoto and he'd lost an eye. The dead eye roamed. It roamed so bad he wore a patch so people wouldn't have to turn away from looking at him. Angel liked to watch the dead eye when the patch was pushed up because the dead eye jumped but when she looked at it Archie always told her, "Shit don't watch it like that, sugar," and slipped the patch down on the eye again. On the Sunday that he cried the tears ran down from underneath the patch as Angel watched. She couldn't understand at first exactly what was happening. Arch had come around before the lamb was in the oven and had seemed like he was going to cry right from the start. Usually he chewed tobacco. Angel saw hc didn't have a bulge inside his cheek so she felt that something strange was going to happen. Her whole life she had never seen a member of her family cry and then this year she'd seen both George and Fanny cry and now it seemed like Arch was going to, too, but first he sat down beside the lamb and breathed real heavy and Angel went on squeezing lemons for the soup and Fanny acted like the lamb that she was dressing was a criminal. Finally Arch began to talk and Angel couldn't understand a word that he was saying except every now and then he said the name "Jeanette" who was his Dot. Then he started saying "George" and started crying so Fanny started shouting at him. "It's all gone to shit," he said in English between sobs to Angel. "George. He shot a man. His hair's turned white. It's all just gone to shit in a straw basket."

That was the first time Angel heard about the hair and it was the first time that she learned that George had killed someone. She had never thought that "shot" and "killed" were words that meant the same before, because "shot" had come to mean the thing she needed to take aim for, but "killed" had always meant to her that something might be dead, but it was jumping.

Sundays changed soon after that. Nichee, Mike and Arch still came to eat but no one shouted and from time to time Arch left the table altogether. Then one Sunday Nick brought two six-packs of malt liquor and the next week Uncle Ray showed up from next door with a pocket full of silver dollars, two unbroken decks of cards and a bottle of Four Roses. He asked Angel to stand beside him as his luck charm, then they let her cut the deck and then Ray told her she could go ahead and sit down on his knee and he wouldn't eat her.

Ray wasn't Angel's uncle like the others were because he wasn't Fanny's son. He was an undertaker and the owner of Gould's Funeral Home next door and it was Ray, not Dr. Brickhouse, who'd taught her how to hold the hypodermic to inject the insulin. Dr. Brickhouse had her practicing on oranges but Ray had let her practice on real skin. He also let her help him out with pancake makeup. Everybody said no one in the Tidewater was equal to Ray Gould with skin tones. Even Nichee's Dot, Cat, who had been in beauty contests and been made up by professionals, said that when it came to helping nature out with pancake makeup Ray was an *artiste* so Angel was real privileged learning tricks from him. Another privilege having Ray next door was the flower arrangements. Once a week Ray brought a floral spray to the back door that he said no one would miss. This was nice especially in winter, even if the flowers spelled out DEAR DEPARTED or, if they didn't, tended to be gladiolas.

EDNA spelled in pink carnations was the centerpiece that Sunday when Ray showed up and the shouting stopped for the next to final time and Angel learned the smell of whiskey and learned a straight takes four of a kind and when a person lies and wins by acting like he isn't lying it's expected and the name for it is bluffing. After a while people got to know where Ray was spending Sunday afternoons and sometimes the phone rang with an emergency because Ray owned the only ambulance in town as well as its two hearses. One Sunday afternoon Angel was wondering what he was up to asking for one card while he was holding nothing but a four and five of the same suit when they got a call from Ned at the police who said there'd been an accident down on City Point and how come they hadn't heard the noise it made all the way up there at the house on North Fourteenth, because it looked like a real doozy. Ray said, "I'm holdin' cards," and Ned said something else then Ray put down the phone and asked Angel if she'd like to take a ride and run the siren. When they got to where the steam was rising off the wrecks on City Point, Ray suddenly said, "Sugar this ain't something you had better see," but Angel got out anyway and followed him and then she wished she hadn't because the ones she'd put the needles into, the ones she'd seen at his place in the basement, had been strangers and this one in the road was Arch's Dot, Jeanette.

They let George out of jail so he could go to Jeanette's funeral but they didn't let him stay around when people went to Archie's house to have a bite to eat after the burial. People brought a lot of food for the occasion and there were lots of olives and dolmathes wrapped for George to take back to the prison with him and although everybody ate a lot Angel noticed Cat had lost a lot of weight and she wasn't eating. She must have come down from a FULL SIZE to a CRIB and she was acting real convivial. "Don't you love my figga?" she asked Angel and made a wobbly pirouette on tippytoe and told Angel to go ahead and try to get her thumb and finger 'round her wrist. "I bet you can slide them right 'round it now," she said, "whereas before you couldn't jam a Hula-Hoop around it." Dot was there too, the real Dot, acting disapproving as if to say that since there were only two Dots left out of the four the real one ought to occupy the higher place because not only was she married to the oldest son but dee oh tee was actually her name. Fanny didn't speak a word to either of them and they acted like they didn't recognize her. What's your point? the slimmed-down Cat, who now actually looked much more like a cat than a big round dot, asked, but it was a formality because clearly Jeanette's jewelry was the only point for miles around so they both pretended that the other things that would begin to collect dust in Arch's life were what the conversation ought to be about so Dot, the real one, said, "There's a lot of this here stuff which needs a one-way straight into the garbage." Like what? Cat said. Corsets, stockings, underwear, Dot answered, and Cat sniffed. Jeanette and Arch had never had a lot of money so Jeanette accumulated only middling things but there were some things she'd inherited and come into the marriage with like two silver brooches, one rhinestone tiara, one fox stole with its head still on, five pearl earrings and some diamonds which could be made to look a lot more decent with reset-ting. Since they didn't want to fight the Dots decided what was fair was to take everything and split it down the middle according to their tastes and in the odd case of the earrings what they'd do was take a pair for each of them and give the odd one out to Angel only Archie, who'd misplaced his patch somewhere since the death, said he wouldn't hear of anything of Jeanette's being thrown out with the garbage and what's more Dot and Cat weren't laying hands on anything of hers because everything was going as it was into boxes to be kept for Angel for that time when she was grown into a woman and could appreciate it. Corsets? Dot demanded, This lil' pole bean of a girl? She got uppity and said, "Well, I guess puttin' it in boxes makes the best sense—after all you might decide you ought to get remarried," whereupon Arch said to Mike he ought to slap restraint onto his wife because Jeanette weren't even cold yet in the ground and then before Mike had a chance to speak Dot said she'd never known such skinflint people who couldn't even keep *pearl earrings* in the family and Archie said she wasn't "family" and she said she'd rather be *dead* than be a relative of his so Archie spit at her then Mike had to spit at him so Archie punched him and Mike punched back then Archie fell against the table with the plate of *koulembiathes* on it and Fanny got five dozen powdered sugar pastries in her black-dressed mourning lap and Nichee threw a punch at Michee because he'd thrown a punch at Archie and everybody in the family started shouting at each other and they all went home in other people's cars claiming that they'd never speak to one another and later that same week Ray got absent-minded and delivered a carnation spray that said JEANETTE and DEARLY MISSED to the back door.

Cat was the next to go, the women disappearing from the family right and left like pocket money, Ray complained. He and Angel were at work on Cat's face on the morning of her funeral when Ray said, "Sugar it's all gone to shit in a straw basket," and she could tell he was torn up. Cat had dropped to ninety-seven pounds and her face was hard to set in any kind of less than skeletal expression, but Ray had got her color almost perfect. If Nick had found her half an hour sooner Ray might have got her to a stomach pump in Richmond in the ambulance because that baby held a hundred miles on dry road like a you-know holds a tit that's why he blamed himself, he said, a lot of deaths don't need to happen when they do.

They let George out of jail so he could go to Cat's funeral and this time they were willing to let him stay around for food but no one got a party up so Ray drove George back to prison in the hearse and then Nick brought a box of Cat's stuff over to the house on North Fourteenth for Angel, including Cat's trophy that she won for Miss Conviviality, and Angel put Cat's stuff with all the other stuff she had from the two other Dots in the suitcase that she kept under her bed. In all the time she'd lived with Fanny she had kept her things inside her suitcase so they'd smell like what had been her parents. The mice had found the artificial leather to their taste and through the years the shiny nylon lining lost all of its aroma but every time she sprang the locks on that old suitcase Angel's heart began to jump. Its existence was a world in which she struggled not to need to live so badly that it made her cry but one she'd like to think she could return to, when she wanted, for a visit. In it there were things that couldn't possibly have meaning when looked at all together by any other person in the world but her and the fact that they articulated no one's losses, no one's history but her own made her feel safe each time she took them out, they made her feel that she was needed. Fanny had a drawer of such things, too, the bottom of the four drawers in the chest of drawers on top of which God lived. Everything inside those drawers smelled like oil and wax except the things inside the bottom drawer. The things inside the bottom drawer smelled sweet and Angel liked the smell of them. In the corner of the bedroom there was a stuffed chair by the window which looked out across the yard over to Ray's funeral home and that's where Fanny sat each evening since her legs had started swelling up. Her feet were blistered and her ankles were both bloated and she couldn't wear her old shoes anymore and the pain of being upright slowed her movements so she spent most afternoons and evenings in the chair with both her legs propped up in front of her. The first time Angel learned about the drawer where Fanny kept her things was when she brought Fanny her meal one night when Fanny had her slippers off and Fanny tried to hide her feet from Angel but Angel wouldn't let her move them 'cause she knew that moving hurt her. Her grandmother's embarrassment embarrassed her, but neither spoke, until Fanny gestured that she wanted something from the chest of drawers. Angel knew the top two drawers held Fanny's clothes and that the third drawer had been cleaned out for her things when she arrived and that except for yellow paper liner it was still completely empty. Angel hadn't ever looked inside the fourth drawer. When she opened it that evening her heart jumped the same way that it did when she unlocked her suitcase. There were things inside which were not beautiful but looked as though they might have been or could be, still, in someone's eyes. There were paper flowers of a dusty color. There was a sort of satin pillow slip and a bit of rusty lace. Near the bottom was a decorated shawl which seemed to be the thing that Fanny wanted. It wasn't until Angel opened it and spread it over Fanny's feet that Angel recognized the shawl. It was the same one in the picture next to God on the chest of drawers, the picture of a young girl in a wedding dress and shawl standing by a young man who is sitting with a high hat in his lap. Angel ran her hand along the cloth to say to Fanny that she thought that it was pretty. Then Fanny touched it, too. Then Fanny told her what it was, or who had made it, or where it came from, or if she'd ever worn it at any other time after her wedding, or what she felt like on her wedding night or what her husband had been like as a young man. Angel didn't understand the words Fanny was telling her so she imagined what her grandmother was saying. When she finished telling Angel all about the shawl Fanny gestured Angel to bring the next thing from the drawer and then she told her a long story about that object, too, and she let Angel hold it while she talked and they passed it back and forth between their hands. By the time the story found its end it was dark and the only light inside the room was from the glass of oil and water where God lived but Angel pulled her suitcase to the middle of the room and snapped the locks and lifted up the lid and sat back on her feet and chose a very special thing which she took to Fanny and let Fanny turn it over in her hands while she explained to Fanny in a foreign language all about where it had come from and who had given it to her and what had happened on that day and what the weather was and what the words were that were spoken. Fanny watched her tell the story as if she understood each thing that Angel said and when Angel had finished speaking Fanny held the object in a new way, Angel thought, she held it in the same way she herself would hold it, with the memory that it provoked. From time to time they took more objects from their secret places and told each other stories. When all the stories had been told Angel set the objects on the floor as if it was a stage then she selected one thing, each, for them to hold and they looked at all their things set out, arrayed before them in the room, the candle flickered and they watched and didn't speak again and each one knew the other one was waiting for a different thing to come and take her.

LONDON
JUNE 1987

MILLIONS

NOW THAT I'VE HAD LUNCH with the Swedish ambassador I can tell you everything you want to know about radioactive reindeer up in Lapland. They feed them to the minks. The reindeer. Yes. The reindeer used to feed the Lapps who depended on them as the native source of protein but now the Lapps feed reindeer to the hungry minks godbless'em on their furry farms because the minks are slaughtered when they're one year old for coats and stoles before they have a chance to die from radioactive reindeer meat. Another fact: There's a lot of lichen up in Lapland: yellow, gray. Radiation from an accident can't kill it. An ac-ci-den-tal-nu-cle-ar-dis-as-ter settles in its veins like spring. Cherryblossomtime, Chernobyl. Want to know what else? Radiation doesn't change its taste. The reindeer up in Lapland eat the lichen 'cause it tastes the same, that's what Lapland reindeer eat. Then they fuck like normal. Experts tell the Lapps that four-to-six-of-every-ten little baby fetal reindeer for the next five generations will simultaneously abort owing to the Accident no sweat they'll feed those four-to-six-of-every-ten spontaneous abortions to little baby minks yum yum that's capitalism. In ten years' time, the Experts say, the herd will be as good as new and Lapps will move the herd once more across the frozen tundra. Is there frozen tundra there in Lapland, sir, or am I dreaming it, I ask. There's everything, I'm told. There are power generators, electricity. There are relay stations for the television. Microwaves. Everything's computerized. I'm told their census is computerized from birth, a phrase which mystifies me, and I'm told by 2010 their nuclear reactor plants will all close down because they've passed a referendum. They'll go back to burning coal. Very very good for Polish miners I am told. But still: don't you fear there will be more Chernobyls, someone from the press corps asks. Well yes, perhaps: and here we're treated to their sense of humor: the ambassador admits it's said in Lapland that there *might* be more but certainly there won't be less.

Some funny: the Embassy's in Portman Place so after lunch I walk down Regent Street and try to catch a bus for home from Piccadilly. I wait half an hour, more or less, I'm not really counting. When a Number 14 finally comes it comes three times in a row a trinity of them, two nearly empty, and when I climb aboard the woman shoving on behind me yells What's the matter with you chaps today? Her hair is the color of old teeth. "What 'chaps'? Do you see 'chaps' before your eyes?" the bus conductor asks. "Listen to me very carefully," he says. "Why are you talking to me about buses? Why don't you talk to Mrs. Thatcher?" Why? I'll tell you why. Mrs. Thatcher doesn't ride the *bus*, that's why, the woman says. "You don't like buses?" the bus conductor says: "Why don't you ride a camel?" You think I haven't ridden camels in my day? the woman booms. Of course I've ridden camels, the children rode them too, we all did, had to, in Karachi. And I'll tell you something else that you don't know, she says. One night a hundred years ago an ancestor of mine got into the wrong bed with the last of the Mogul kings so I've got plenty of your kind of blood in my veins so don't make idle chat to me—! " 'Idle chat'? Do you hear 'idle chatting' in your ears?" he asks. *You are speaking very loudly* they are told by a bald man with a German accent. Why *not*? the woman wants to know. It's not Polite, she's told. " 'Polite'?" the bus conductor shouts. I am a taxi driver in my country, says the accented man, and never do we speak to strangers with such loudness. Don't you lecture *me* about Politeness, he is scolded by the woman, Don't you try to lecture *me* in any German accent, he is told. Oh boy, I think: it's time for me to walk, when suddenly would you believe it, there goes Fozi making like a bandit out the front door of the London Park Tower Casino in broad daylight. In Knightsbridge. But I mean *running*. Hey, I think. He looks like he's afraid of being shot. Ol' Foz for christsake! haven't seen him for at least a year and here he is running I mean *running* down the street in a pinstripe suit toward the taxi rank around the corner in Seville Street. It was him alright, there was never mistaking Fozi in a crowd, that head of his, his hair. Before I can get off the bus I see this puffy red-faced flunky in a pearl gray vest and morning coat explode from the casino bearing crumpled paper in his right hand, looking right, then left. He looks up toward Hyde Park Corner then he looks down toward Harrod's then back up toward Apsley House again. He's wearing a pale lemon tie, color of Béarnaise, and he's astonishingly puffy, like a pudding or an adder in a lather: I think, Next he's going to call the cops. Do they call the cops, these guys? Next he's going to call on law enforcement. What did the ol' Foz do? I wonder. Crazy Foz. Born to gamble samba and seduce. A party in a pinstripe suit all by his crazy self, party of one, making a quick getaway in a taxi down Seville Street while the well-dressed flunky stands there in a froth with these two other evil-looking guys. "Now I'm going to tell you something, listen to me very very carefully," the bus conductor says. "Who are you to talk to *us* about Politeness?"

Next day I come out my door and two guys in too-straight suits are standing there so I go back in. They start beating on my door. Maybe only one of them is beating and maybe only one of them is beating with only one fist but the sound he makes with it isn't anything except only awfully frightening. Who's there? I ask. Immigration. I don't need any, I say. You better open up, they say. I open up a peek. Are you Simon Fishbine? they ask me. Do I *look* like Simon Fishbine? I say. We'd like to have a word with him. He doesn't live here, I inform them. No? Where does he live then? On the Riviera. Are you his wife? I'm not. Girlfriend? No. Are you related to him? No. Who are you then? they ask.

Lord Curzon coined this little euphemism back in India a century ago called "right of portico" because he had one, see. A portico. Some people he allowed to come up to his door beneath his portico and others he left standing at the gates. I left these guys standing at the gates. Which is swell except they stood there all that day and all that night and all the next day until noon when I had to go out finally 'cause I needed to buy some water. Why don't you level with us sweetie, they say. About the telephone. It's listed in this Fishbine's name at this address and somebody by the name of Fausto Mahmet known as Fozi has been making frequent calls to it. We want some information. Shoot, I say. Do you know this person Simon Fishbine? Oh him, yeah—he's my landlord. Do you know this person Fausto Mahmet? Maybe. It's a common name. There are quite a few. We're looking for him, they inform me.

That night Fozi calls me from his favorite Chinese restaurant. Foz, the feds are after you, I say. Oh you Americans, he says. Always so busy busy. Come and have some lobster with black bean sauce, he suggests. It's midnight, I remind him. Fresh lobsters, he says, special fresh. Swimming right now in the tank with little seaweeds. Sorry, Foz, I say. An hour, yes? I'll wait one hour. You'll change your thinking and you'll come. I've put my powers on you.

Such a lot of powers—I go to bed and sleep the sleep of Innocence. In the morning there's a message on my answering machine. Thank you very much, it says. I waited for you many hours. After that my angerness made me go lose a million pounds at the cazino.

So I get dressed and go out. How I met Fozi: I got dressed one morning in September and went out. City of London. Rode the Number 105 bus from Shepherd's Bush to Southall and got off at Western Avenue to wander through the markets. Went into a restaurant I found there called the Brilliant. It was crowded. A man was sitting at a table in the corner, arguing with moneylenders. It was Fozi. He had the largest head I've ever seen on any human being outside Nancy Reagan. He came up to me and said I've put my powers on you, You are mine. He owned five ships, he said, under Libyan registry and he ran rice and oil from Limassol to Rio. I have paid your bill, he told me. The next few weeks whole taxiloads of fruit, guavas were his specialty, arrived at my front door in Chelsea every other day. But by then he'd started gambling, again. Or maybe he had never stopped.

I walk to Earl's Court, bent on riding on the Piccadilly Line to Arnos Grove just for the fun of it. A busker playing saxophone which echoes through the Underground extracts the loose change from my pocket. On the Tube there are no empty seats. Standing with a pole between us on a ride which makes us rattle in a dance a woman wrapped in bright blue cotton asks me When am I do come- o na Harrod's? Three stops, I say, and hold up three fingers. She counts on her wrist, her elbow and her shoulder one two three. Oh hell, I think: get out at Knightsbridge, girl, and make for Hyde Park where there are things still growing like real flowers. On the Brompton Road I run into three Arab women wrapped in black silk scarves, their noses and their mouths masked too, covening before Kutchinsky's jeweler's window, coveting the diamonds so I cross the road. Across the road there is a big display of fur coats for next winter. Lots of fox and lots of sable. Lots of mink. Goll-ee, I hear somebody say. How much you think a coat like that must cost? I turn around. Before I have a chance to ask them if they're over here for a vacation I hear the woman answer Gosh. You mean if it's real. The mink. I reckon. Who knows? Honey? *Millions*.

LONDON
MAY 1985

COUNTING

MILDRED KNOWS THE TWO THINGS are related and she sometimes wonders who the boy was who got her started on this venture and she hopes he isn't dead. Mildred hates to hear about dead children. More than Mildred hates to hear about dead pregnant women, even, Mildred hates to get the news about dead kids. She hates to hear about sick kids, too, but no one ever tells you numbers with the sick, they just talk about specific symptoms. Loss of weight. Dyspepsia. You never read THREE THOUSAND SICK KIDS COUNTED IN SAVANNAH, but you read TWO YOUNGSTERS' BODIES FOUND. They never give you numbers with the sick. They never say, "His temperature was ninety-nine at bedtime, but it dropped to normal in his sleep as he began to sweat." Instead they say, "The body had four stab wounds and there's evidence of sexual wrongdoing." The only time they give specifics of sick and injured kids is when there's been abuse. "Anus" is a word they like to write: "frequent" and "enlarged." They never write, "When he had his fever he dreamed they made him ride a Ferris wheel. He dreamed his soul fell from his pockets." Instead they write, "The victim had been robbed."

She remembers the precise moment that she began to count. She was in her car, driving from the supermarket, minutes after she had met the boy whose father pushed him in a supermarket cart. Other things had happened to her, too, in supermarkets in her lifetime. She had met the nice man Damien she dated several years, she had met him in a U-Krops. She had saved a person's life once, in a Safeway. She had been the only one to say, "Stand back, give him air!" and they had told her later it had saved his life. It was in a supermarket she had realized for the first time she would never marry. And sometimes in a supermarket, Foodtown mostly, she would freeze up, have a sort of seizure as it dawned on her how much she loved the land. Land was Mildred's way of saying "Life." Instead of dawning on her she was glad to be alive, that she loved Life, Mildred's thinking thing, her mind, deceived her into thinking what she loved was land. Not any land. This one. From sea to shining. Sweet Virginia. Home of. Tennessee. The brave.

The Mississippi River made her weep. When she saw it on TV it brought on tears and tightness in her throat. Jack Kerouac wrote the Mississippi smells the way it does because it bathes the nation. Mildred never knew Jack Kerouac, she was born ten years before him and from what is said about him she suspects she'd never been his kind of person, what Mildred calls a woo woo. Misconceptualized. But if Jack were still alive he'd still be ten years younger, that's how history works. Numbers fall in history's grooves and stay there, can't escape, like sound on vinyl records. Mildred knows that laser discs don't work that way. The sound goes on and lasts about a dozen years and then begins to disappear. Mildred learned this in a Supersave. Standing by the serve yourself a salad bar. A man walked up with wires in his ears and Mildred said, "Don't touch this, son, I saw them spray it so it looks alive." He didn't seem to hear her so she stage whispered advice into the round thing in his ear because she thought it was a hearing aid. Man's name was Kobayashi, Sony salesman, and he made her try his Discman. Mildred thought her teeth were going to come unglued. The stone the angel guarded by the cave inside her skull rolled back revealing Sony god of man. Beethoven, his music, was inside her head. Not just on her skin, like music at a concert, or in her ears like music from the radio: this was music in her head and louder, too, than anything she'd ever heard. "You love it?" Kobayashi asked. She answered that she loved the land. Then he showed her how the Discman works and what the disc looks like. "You have to love it," Kobayashi said. "Sound was made to be this way."

Perhaps this introduction to the way that sound was meant to be knocked numbers loose in Mildred's grooves, because it was the week after meeting Mister Kobayashi at the Supersave that she met the boy whose father pushed him in the supermarket cart at the A&P. Maybe they had started, numbers, well before she met the boy. Maybe all the numbers had been there, in her ears or on her skin like lint, but never in her head the way that sound had never been, until she'd heard the way that sound was meant to be, from Mister Kobayashi's Discman. In two more years she would be eighty. Imagine living all those years not knowing sound you heard was not the sound the way that sound was meant to be, not knowing sound was something found not in your ears or on your skin, but that sound was something you could only hear, or really hear, from Sony. After Discman, Mildred started to discount, perhaps. She was not a stupid woman. She knew that certain substances, radio-activities, isotopes they're called, exist, in theory, for eternity and own a property called half-life, the time it takes for half the element to decompose. Some elements, like silver, do not decompose. Those elements are stable. Other elements decompose at different rates toward half-life, then they have their half-lives measured in the books by seconds (s), minutes (m), hours (h), days (d) or years. The half-life of plutonium, for example, is 24,400 years. Just trying to imagine something going on that long, especially death—what else could you call what follows after half-life has been reached?—made Mildred dizzy. To think she had spent all her life so far not knowing about sound. What else was there that she had missed by halves. What else was there she hadn't totaled to its full.

Maybe she was thinking about this when she showed up at the A&P for milk because as soon as she got to the dairy aisle she knew something was wrong. This was not the dairy aisle where she was used to buying milk. This was a long, abundant dairy aisle. A foreign one. Could she be confused? Wasn't it at A&P where milk was sold? Was it only sold at Acme? Mildred looked at all the cartons. At the plastic jugs. Half-pint size, pint size, quart, half-gallon, single-serving, gal., 2 gal., gallon and a ½. A-added, B-added, A- and D-added, semi-skimmed, skimmed, soy-substitute, chocolate-flavored, liquid yogurt, berry-flavored, full-fat, protein-added, light-and-lively, butter-, full-cream, half-cream, half-and-half. There was a button there, under a sign which indicated, PRESS FOR SERVICE. She pressed it and a youth in a white coat appeared beside her in a little while. "Hi," he said. "Can I help?"

"I'm looking for some milk," said Mildred.

"Milk," he said.

"Plain milk."

He nodded.

"I've bought it here before," she lied.

The youth engaged her in a full-face look.

Nothing ½ about it.

Raised his arm.

"What's the prob?" he posed.

He waved his raised arm down the aisle.

"Can't find it," Mildred said.

The youth assumed an attitude of empathy.

"You mean, like, milk," he said.

They looked at all the different types of milk together.

"You mean, like, from a cow."

For an instant Mildred wondered if the boy had ½ a brain.

"You mean, with nothing in it."

"Yes."

He said he thought they had some in the back.

Not too many people asked for it.

He disappeared.

When he returned he held a plastic jug that had a label on it that said RAW MILK with the date. Nonpasteurized, non FDA-approved, the raw and clotty stuff straight from the udder.

Just then a man pushing a cart with a young boy riding in the part where Mildred liked to place her purse and pressure-perishable produce such as raspberries (in season) came down the aisle and paused beside them while the man considered milk. The boy was four or five years old. "And one time, Dad," the boy said in a loud and ringing voice, "another old lady came and counted to two hundred without getting sick." The man selected a half-gallon of the semi-skimmed, then he pushed away. Mildred told the youth in the white coat that what he had there in his clutches was most likely an illegal substance, that never in her life, and she was seventy-eight years old, had she encountered unsterilized milk for sale in a certified environment other than some slop shop whose specialty was cheese guaranteed to have a longer fuller life than a lot of infants born in Mexico and even in the Third World there were health controls regarding milk, its sterilization et cetera, and she had a good mind to march right out and take it up before the Board of Health, in fact that was exactly what she thought she'd do, imagine. Keeping it out back like homemade hootch.

Outrage got her through the door out to the parking lot,

inside her car. The radio came on with the ignition. While she was turning from the lot into the four-lane traffic down Route Ten, the news began. "A twenty-one-year-old man was murdered in a drive-by shooting in downtown Richmond this morning, police report."

One, thought Mildred.

"In Pakistan, more than two hundred and fifty people have been killed in the past ten days. On Sunday ten people were killed including an army captain and two militiamen in shootouts with Sindhi bandits."

Mildred made a silent tally.

"The Kremlin has reported that at least forty persons have died in three days of ethnic rioting in the Central Asian republic of Kirghizia."

Need a pencil, Mildred thought.

She pulled into a 7-Eleven and bought the *New York Times*, the *Washington Post* and the *Richmond Times Dispatch*. The New York paper cost a fortune but it had more numbers in it than the other two. She bought a yellow legal pad and a box of six lead pencils. Should I only count the names or should I count the bodies, Mildred wondered. She remembered to buy milk. For tea. ½ pint with D-added.

She decided to count names and bodies.

One list for the ones with names.

One list for the unnamed bodies.

One day in September when a plane went down she counted four hundred and eighty-two with names.

She bought a map.

She worked a system out with colored pins.

White pin (w) for a place where only one was killed. Blue pin (b) for a place taking less than twenty. Green pin (g) for places up to fifty. Yellow (y) for places (Osh was one) where a hundred unnamed people were reported to have died.

At the end of May something happened in the world,

some oversight, an unaccountable caesura, on a single day, the same day, no deaths were reported on the front pages of each of the five papers she read daily (she had started buying the *Baltimore Sun* and the *Philadelphia Inquirer*, paid for by the money that she saved not buying milk).

She pinned the pages to her wall around the map. She bought silver-colored pins for the occasion.

Then, before the first bright week of June was over, Mildred saw the headlines about Janet Adkins. Mildred saw her picture, too.

She stopped counting for a while.

Took to bed the middle of the afternoon.

Took the map and pages off the wall.

When she took the map down there were drips there, on the wall, she'd never seen before.

Once, when she was sixty-eight, she'd slipped and fallen in the snow and they had had to set her hip. They put a drip into her arm and wheeled her backwards down a corridor. Don't you worry they told Mildred. Have you fixed in no time dear, they said. Everywhere we count more and we value less. A slogan, Mildred thought. She was feeling easy, light. The dripping. Mildred, nod if you can hear me, good. Can you hear me, Mildred? I want you to start counting to a hundred, please. By twos. What else? Mildred could remember thinking. World was saved by twos. No ah, no problem. She'd been feeling lovely, all those drips. Man had such a lovely voice, that lovely voice, all members of his sex and his profession should. Lovely voices, lovely hands. Of course, ever since she had discovered she'd heard sound falsely all her life, by halves, she could hardly say how lovely his, the doctor's, voice must have been to those equipped to really hear it. Maybe in the future we will all be Discmen. Better hearing, Mildred thought. Equal opportunity for all. No more deafness, only Discmen. Music. Compositions. No more decomposing. No more half-lives. Only lovely hands.

This doctor in the suburb of Detroit didn't look to Mildred like he had such lovely hands. He looked the part, as the *Richmond Times Dispatch* reported, of someone who had once proposed "that Death Row prisoners be made permanently unconscious and used for medical experiments." A pathologist. Apologist. A pathologically half man. I wonder what he said to Janet Adkins, Mildred thought. Have you fixed in no time, dear? "Suicide device," the Richmond paper called his gizmo. Why don't we call our spades our spades? thought Mildred. Name the things that dig the graves for what they are. What's a semiautomatic weapon? One that isn't fully automatic? Is it automatic in its function by a ½? This device this doctor used on Janet Adkins was a semiautomatic one as well. It consisted of three jars, the papers said, three containers—one full-size, two ½, connected to a drip tube which he put into her arm. The large container held a "harmless saline solution," the New York paper said and Mildred had to wonder, with her half a life of teaching chemistry, what's a harmful one? The two small jars held chemicals she'd never heard of. Sodium thiopental. The Philadelphia paper said it was a "substance that induced unconsciousness." The *Post* described the other chemical, potassium chloride, as a solution "which stops the heart and brings death on in minutes." All Janet Adkins had to do was press a button which switched the intake in her veins from saline in the full-size jar to sodium thiopental in the half-. Then, after several minutes, the gizmo switched the intake automatically from sleeping potion to the death solution. What a clever semiautomatic, Mildred thought. Let me count the ways. Earthquake in Rumania. Stray bullet, man killed in his bathroom while he shaves, from ricocheting fire in the street below. Pilot sucked through airplane window. AIDS. I wonder what he said, this doctor in the suburb of Detroit. As Janet went so lightly through those stages into death. The *Sun* reported, "Just before she died, he said, 'She looked at me with grateful eyes and said, "Thank you, thank you, thank you." ' " Yes, Mildred thought, but what did *you* say? What does anybody say. She woke me up and so I killed her. I was in a sort of trance. It was like we never saw it coming. Shoot the nonbeliever, go to heaven. Warned him not to fuck with me. Told him not to come. Go on try it sucker. Make my day. I'm sorry. Start at zero. Janet? She was fifty-four. The papers said she had Alzheimer's. The papers said she was a teacher. Today we'll start with history, children. Start with zero. Now go backwards.

LONDON
JUNE 1990

A CUP OF JO

LIGHT STRIKING WATER in the vase of branches casts a sundog on the pale green blotter on the old man's desk and he is halfway through the letter he is writing when it dawns on him the friend to whom this letter is addressed is gone. He's dead, this friend. This friend of his who'd like this letter, how could he forget? Well, sure: too long ago to be remembered, nothing left to do but stop but still he'd like to finish. He'd like to feel as full of news as when he started it, he'd like to have that news a rainbow on his mind, to see it clearly as this pot here on this dotter. Pesk. This spot here on this blotter on his desk. This . . . *pen*! yes. This what this *pen* this instrument: This water dropping down.

Saying something: What's she saying? Doesn't know how young she is. She doesn't know how young a thing can look in what's this instance sort of thing that dances, *daylight*:

"Uncle Harry?" she is saying, "you've been crying. Do you understand? These words? You're crying. Here. Your tears are falling down. You've made your paper wet, see?

Here: You're crying. Tears. These things are tears: Now. You've been crying. Can you tell me why you're crying: Harry? Try."

. . . Fry: a hundred of them. Joey. *Trout*!

"Oh, *I* see—you've made a picture. May I see it? Harry? What you've drawn?"

This is Joey's fetter.

. . . *Letter*!

"Oh, it's pretty. Harry: Hold it up. It's very pretty. Am I right to think you've drawn a fish?"

Yes! a *dish* . . .

The stream.

"And such a pretty fish, what kind of fish are we supposed to call this, Harry? What name are we supposed to give it? Is it a goldfish? Harry? Is it *a whale*?"

. . . the color of intestines:

This. Is. Something. Fish. *Thisisatrout*.

"Is it a fish you want someone to cook for dinner? Harry?"

Catch. It is a *fish*. Snake River. Jo.

"Or am I wrong to ask if it's a fish at all," she wonders.

"Can you try to tell me why this drawing makes you cry?" she asks.

. . . its freckles:

Speckled!

God that kind of blue.

"Does this picture make you think of something sad?"

Tent? No: brown canvas. Camping on Snake River, me and Jo, the ground is damp. Wet leaves. Pine needle smell. Big moon, the moon is big. It's moonlight. *We've been lucky ain't we* Joey says. He's talking weather. *Always are* I say. And then he ticks off all those names: those stars.

"What is it, Harry—Look. Here. You shouldn't cry like this. You're crying. Can you try and tell me why you're crying?"

Sky so blue: two men fishing, casting arcs like welders, equal weights, the river cast as fulcrum in their lives' mechanics . . .

"That's why I'm here, you know," she says, "for you to talk. So you can talk to me. Remember?"

Sitting on the shore: Joey pulling on his boots, his saying *Harry, I dreamed last night I had a conversation with the Infinite* and my looking over at him, asking Well what'd it have to say forgodsake, Jo?

Not. One. Word, he says.

So how'd you have a conversation with it if it didn't say a word? I ask him. Joey?

"Uncle Harry?"

Jo?

. . . into water to our waists before the dawn, our oilcloths insulating us against the cold, as if we were night's larvae spawned inside bright bubbles: Fry were slapping! Early light. Before the stroke, the *strike*: small fry, at least a thousand of them. Slow steam rising off fast water. There were a thousand of them then . . . *Well I'll be damned*! shouts Joey: *strike*! the arc! the line! the net, bright water then that kind of blue that belly. Water cold and sharp around my wrists the trout's own element, like cuffs: cold water like a razor if I slip, then Joey by the fire fingers purple with the cold his knuckles white around that cup that smell of something kestrel pinned against a cloud behind his shoulder *Harry* he was saying laughing *what a morning*! that aroma rising steamy something got the word now, *Harry: what a cup of jo*

MARTHA'S VINEYARD
AUTUMN 1981

CROESO I GYMRU

WE WERE ON THE LAM IN WALES, running through the Black Mountains like unarmed smugglers from the righteous with their guns. Everywhere we went there were slate tombstones, upright shadows, on the hills. In the towns there were slate houses, with slate roofs. There was darkness, dead as coal, behind the windows of the houses. There were ravens in the fields and on the roads. English words from a Welsh poet seemed to sit on the horizon like an advertisement for the land: *This sad distracted abstract of my woe*. The mountains wore a beard of snow, even as the pussy willows in the valleys bloomed. Pussy willow trees in Wales are called "goat" willows, I found out, because goats like to eat their leaves. Only the male trees with their yellow catkins are called "pussy." Where we'd found a hideout for a while, there was a male goat willow tree in bloom that I looked onto from my window. I cut some of its branches for a jar that I placed in the window in the kitchen of the house but then the catkins, turning golden, made me sneeze. I found out about the "goat" name for the tree from a book called *Trees of Britain* that I'd found on the bookshelf in the kitchen next to cookbooks and some novels by Alistair MacLean. That's how I knew about the catkins but I didn't know what "catkin" meant. I looked it up in the dictionary that I always travel with. Anyone who knows me knows that I can't spell. I have to keep a dictionary with me within reach even for something so simple as writing a letter. There are times when I can't spell *Sincerely*. At home, where we used to live, I had a dictionary handy in each room. Now I have a single one and good thing, too—the people who are with us now depend on it for Scrabble. A "catkin," I can tell you, is an inflorescence. I depend on books for meaning. I depend on them for definition. A "catkin" is a thing defined as "a reduced flower of either sex." Following the definition of "catkin" in my dictionary there was the advice, "See *ament*." I didn't feel like seeing *ament*. Instead I watched the thaw of snow across the tops of mountains. The Welsh say when there's snow on mountains it's an indication there'll be more. I learned that from a book about Welsh legends. Eventually I did "See *ament*" and its definition was "another word for *catkin*." Its second definition, *ament II*, was "Noun. *Psychiatry*. A mentally deficient person." Next to the houses built of plastered-over slate along the roads, the houses with dark windows, there were hedgerows, yews and daffodils. No kitchen gardens grew. A kitchen garden—chamomile, dill, parsley, carrots, rue—is an English affectation: in Wales the land around a house is purely land, no frippery, no spices grown. The potato did not root in Wales until a century post-Raleigh and even in the middle of the eighteenth century at the Aberystwyth market, potatoes, price per pound, were as expensive as the local cheese. Oats were what the Welsh ate, in a porridge they called *bwdran*. *Cawl*, a vegetable hot pot with potatoes and a bit of bacon or a sheep joint added to it, is the traditional dish in Wales. Sheep are the common stock. Walking up on a hill one morning I found a sheep skull, embedded in the earth beside a corkscrew holly. Sheep were everywhere. We laughed sometimes: called the scenery The Big Sheep. On days when I could walk, when it wasn't pelting hail or rain or snowing, on days when they allowed me to, I walked and walked, walked straight up sheer hills out of anger, up over turfy lichen-strewn terrain punctuated now and then by those wind-bleached sheep skulls beached like whelks, and by fox holes and those twisted holly trees surprising the horizon. Above me at about two feet at scarifying intervals: jump jets: a Harrier's harangue: RAF: unmarked: some of them dark green and some of them with red and white striped bellies. These were the Hunters, I learned. And I learned other things: That a sheep can recognize another sheep but can't differentiate between a horse and human. That a swede is a rutabaga and is used for cattle fodder. That sheep eat beetroots and molasses. That great tracts of Wales are designated by Great Britain solely for the practice of war games. Near where we were hiding there was an MOD training camp where paratroopers trained. Young men in green track suits with the information COMBAT '89 stenciled on their sweatshirts practiced calisthenics in our road and military Land Rovers outnumbered every other sort of vehicle I saw. I was afraid I would be recognized and once a military Land Rover passed me on our road and slowed down and stopped and waited and I took off, changed direction and headed back across the meadows. When I told this to the people that we have to live with now they told me that it wasn't that the person in the Land Rover had identified me as the person who I am but that he had identified me *as a woman*. The people that we have to live with now have taught me a few things about an all-male camp: they like to look at women. Men do. So I'm told. Then once, too, I thought the woman in the health food store in the market town I shopped in had recognized me owing to the way she stared at me. But the people that we have to live with now told me that she stared at me, most likely, because I have an accent. One of the people that we live with now asked me when he came to us the first time, "Say, do you know Neil Schreiber?" No, I said. Who's Neil Schreiber? "Chap I know. American. He has an accent just like yours. I thought maybe you knew him." *But in my village* I was tempted to reply *there are eight hundred million people.* Another one of the people that we have to live with now told me that when his wife, who's Thai, came to live in England she thought the sheep were a foreign breed of dog. There were so many sheep where we were hiding that 100,000 were stolen last year around the town of Brecon. Brecon is a market town. At the Brecon market there were: barren cows, fat bulls, fat ewes, fat hoggets, weaned calves, breeding cows, bulling heifers, cull bulls, pedigree beef bulls and rams. I learned this by reading local papers. While we were in hiding I read the papers, local ones, like someone on a river, like that someone, the colonel, in Garcia Marquez's story who reads the papers that come on the boat once a week, out-of-date papers from elsewhere, he reads every word of them, chronologically, front to back, everything, even the ads. The local paper that I looked forward to the most was published every week, on Thursdays. Thursdays, then, held definite excitement. The paper cost twenty-four pence. No other journal—not the *New York Times* nor the *Washington Post* nor the *Guardian*—was more looked forward to by me during those weeks than the *Brecon-Radnor Express & Powys County Times*, sixteen pages every week. It was through that weekly that I learned location, began to find out where I was and who the people were that sometimes passed by me on the road. I was not allowed to hold a conversation with a stranger. The question *Are you staying in the village?* when I went into a store one day to buy some coal to fire the stove which heated the house where we were hiding prevented me from ever going back. I was the

American—Americans around those parts were few. Why was I there? What was my purpose? The coal stove in the kitchen was a Bosky. I learned about the different kinds of anthracite that one can buy. I learned why many of the sheep are painted colors—coded blue, magenta, orange, like flashcards on the hills; carded wool. One color means they've lambed, another means the ram has visited. *Dafad* is the Welsh word meaning sheep, and *dyfodol* is the Welsh word meaning future. I know this because in Brecon one day I bought a dictionary and a book called *Welsh for Learners*. I needed to find out about the daffodils, I wanted to find out how they, the daffodils, became a symbol of the Welsh. I knew about the leek, because a leek is on pound coins. There are three imprints of pound coins in Great Britain: one of them is English, one of them is Scottish, one is Welsh. All bear the Queen's profile on one side, although on the English and the Scottish coins her image is much younger-looking than the image on the Welsh. The Scottish pound coin has a thistle, verso, a thistle set inside a crown. Around the edge of the Scottish version there's the motto NEMO ME IMPUNE LA-CESSIT: *no one touches me without unpleasant consequences*. On the verso of the English one there's the coat of arms of England and a lot of French—HONI SOIT QUI MAL Y PENSE and DIEU ET MON DROIT—and around the edge of it there are the Latin words DECUS ET TUTAMEN. On the Welsh pound coin there's a fancy leek, looking like a fleur-de-lis, with its stem stuck through a crown just like the Scottish thistle. Around its edge are etched the words PLEIDIOL WYF I'M GWLAD. I needed to find out what *pleidiol wyf i'm gwlad* meant. Its meaning became a sort of test, a sort of project to me. My days were filled with projects: one day I cooked a swede, for instance. It seemed to take forever. One day, too, I cataloged the differences among the sorts of lichen I had found. One day I tried to learn about the game of rugby. I made a project out of watching birds for about a minute every other day, or when I saw an interesting, bright-colored one. A hatch, or something—blue, and yellow-breasted—liked to feed on certain catkins in the tree outside my window, and I learned the border-country legend about 1 magpie brings you rotten luck but when you see two magpies on the wing together you're going to get a treat. So every time you see a single magpie you're supposed to say, "Where's your mistress, Mister Magpie?" and the magpie is assumed to answer, *By my side but you can't see her.* One day we got a letter from a friend in Canada whose eight-year-old daughter wrote to say that she was working on a project about blinking. This was a subject that I filed away for future use. In the meantime I had learned that *plismon* is the Welsh word for policeman. But as for *pleidiol wyf i'm gwlad*: I was having trouble cracking it. *Gwlad*, I found out, means "country." But the rest, the other words . . . the closest I could come to *pleidiol* was *pledio*, the verb which means "to plead." In hiding, as I was, the signs, the symbols, slogans, took on added meaning: I remembered a short story by Paul Bowles in which some Buddhists in (back then) Ceylon ask some Western gentlemen whom they encounter on a bus about the meaning of the stripes and colors of their ties. What did the stripes and colors signify? Why did some men wear ties while others not? *Who can believe the story? Who can remember? What's reasonable these days?*: these were sample questions from the book I bought called *Welsh for Learners. What's cooking in the oven? Who's perfect? What's in the soil? What's better than this? Who was collecting stones? Who had been crying? Which ones had failed? Who cleaned the edges?* Some sample sentences employing the conditional were, "We could have purposely deceived them." "I should have taken the bitter medicine." "The woman should have suffered it." "They should pay half at least." I liked especially the Welsh expression *yn eich elfen* which means "in your element," *elfen* meaning "element" but sounding small, manlike and mischievous. I made a project of learning to translate Welsh placenames. I'd grown up in Pennsylvania never knowing that Bryn Mawr is Welsh for "big hill." I made a project of Welsh sounds. *Bŵl* is easier to say when you know that it's the word for bull; when you know that *bwcl* is the word for buckle, *bŵm* for boom, *bwlb* for bulb; *bwrdd sgôr*, scoreboard; *bwrdd sbring*, a trampoline. *Llanfairpwllgwyngyllgogerchwyrndrobwllllantysiliogogogoch* is the longest placename on the map. What the name means is "Saint Mary's Church of the pool of the white hazel near the rushing whirlpool of Saint Tysylw's Church, near the red cave." *What's a red cave?* I wrote down in my notebook: *what makes it red?* I kept trying to make sense from nothing. What is the name of that bird? I kept thinking to myself *what if these are the limits of life, what if this is the all of what is?* Once a month the *Brecon-Radnor Express* had a page called "W.I. News." "W.I.," I found out, stood for Women's Institute. Women's Institute was the name of a club, a service club, and hundreds of them were scattered through Wales. Once a month on the "W.I." page, page eight, I could read the reports from the clubs in the county—from Three Cocks and Llanwrtyd and Aberhonddu and Bwlch and Defynnog and Garth. *A pleasant half-hour was spent looking at local and holiday slides taken by members which proved to be very interesting. Japan is densely populated but Mrs. Scutt saw no litter and found the people polite and friendly. Mrs. Ursula Pumphrey proposed a vote of thanks* . . . From Crickhowell: "The competition, a Valentine verse based on bread, was won by Mrs. Freda Jones." From Bluith Wells: "The competition 'Most Artistically Folded Napkin' was won by Mrs. Dilys Jones." From Penderyn: "The competition 'The Most Unusual Teapot' was won by Mrs. Cooke." From Llangasty: "Refreshments were served and there followed a 'social time,' organized by Mrs. Wendy Griffith, during which members had some fun demonstrating how ambidextrous they were." From Garth: "The competition was for the longest apple peel." From Defynnog: "The competition for the most unusual button was." From Glasbury: "The competition for an unusual pebble was." From Tretower: "Competition winners for the best covered coat-hanger were." There was an article one week called "From Sheep to Shells" about a woman in the Brecon hills who had decided that her small holding could not provide her with a decent living raising sheep so she had sold them and invested in a one-hundred-breeder-strong conurbation of land snails, African ones, said to be more tender and less rubbery than their North European cousins. It was by reading this article that I learned that the African land snail gestates in four months as compared to two years for the European species, and that Eastern European snails have been contaminated, anyway, ever since Chernobyl. It was in the *Brecon-Radnor Express*, too, that I read that "A farmer who staggered into a neighbor's house half naked, covered in blue dye with his hands and testicles bound with rubber bands has been cleared of the charges that he planted a hoax bomb and wasted police time . . . Stephen Gilmore Williams said that he had crossed two fences with his hands tied behind his back and his testicles bound in a rubber band but Det Inspector D A Davies of Ammanford had tried to do the same but had failed to do so." ONLY JESUS SAVES I saw one day painted on a railroad bridge when we were driving somewhere on the run near Merthyr Tidfyl, and the *plismon* in my company remarked, "Not on our bloody pensions Jesus couldn't." WALES IS NOT FOR SALE I saw painted on some rocks in the Black Mountains. I learned that there had been an increase in the incidence of arson, that Welsh nationalists were setting fire to the summer homes owned by the English. And there was murder, too. And racial violence. From the *Express* I learned about the findings of an inquest—JURY RETURN VERDICT THAT YOUTH WHO DIED IN RIVER PLUNGE WAS UNLAWFULLY KILLED—into the death of a twenty-year-old boy from Trenewydd, Llanfaes, who had fallen twenty feet from the Llanfaes Bridge in Brecon into the

River Usk the previous December. A Home Office pathologist had found that the deceased had died of brain damage resulting from a fractured skull. She, the doctor, had discovered no evidence of drowning. The report, which I read in my room in my place of hiding, said, "Passing Christ College the two defendants, who were quite merry by then, began singing a Max Boyce song about the English not being able to raise a rugby team to beat the Welsh. It was fairly rude, they added." *Who's Max Boyce?* I wrote down in my notebook. It was the forty-seventh item on my list of things to find out, my list of things to learn and do. Number 46 was *Try to get a copy to re-read Hal IV, Part I, re: OWEN GLENDOWER.* Number 45, crossed out, had been *Find out the diff betw SCREE and SLAG.* "As they were a quarter way across Llanfaes Bridge, still singing," the article continued, "a witness noticed two other youths on the opposite side of the bridge who were carrying paper-wrapped portions of fish and chips and eating from them. 'Because we thought we might have offended them,' the defendants said, 'we shouted, "*Are you English?*" ' Then all of a sudden, they testified, the blond-haired person charged across the bridge and grabbed one of them by the collar and was abusive towards him calling him 'a wanker.' Aware that the other person, the deceased, had come across the bridge as well, one of the defendants testified, 'Something caught my eye and I saw him against the railings. He flipped over backwards over the bridge. The whole incident happened within seconds.' At the outset of his summing up, the coroner told the jury what verdicts they could consider appropriate to return. The choices facing them, he said, were a) unlawful killing, b) accidental death or death by misadventure, and c) an open verdict." "Unlawful killing," the article went on to teach me, "means manslaughter or murder." *What's an "open verdict"?* I wrote down. I looked it up. An open verdict is a finding by a coroner's jury of death without stating the cause.

Death by unstated causes: Death by death, in other words. *Marw* is the word in Welsh that translates "dead." It sounds like *mort*, when spoken. *Marwoldeb* is the word that means "mortality"; *marwol* is the word for "lethal"; *marwor* is the word for cinder, a dead fire. One night, watching news from elsewhere on the television, I saw the president of a bankrupt desert nation speak into a microphone while an English-accent male voice-over translated his, the president's, intent to send a black arrow of revenge from that distant desert into my husband's heart. We were hiding in a Legendary place, a place where Legends grew-from-ground, Arthurian, Tolkeinate. To learn to write was an ancient Celtic fear, an accomplishment charged with retribution and with danger. Caesar, encountering the Celts, judged their belief to be that knowledge, rite, wisdom, rune—those who could write of those things held power, those who could write of the arcane, of rite and of worship, were people who deserved to be, who must be feared. Hiding one's name, never writing it down, never committing one's name into symbol, is still a recurring motif in Welsh legends and stories. It's still dangerous to put one's name on paper. *Mae'r dial drosodd* speaks the Legendary Welsh voice, rising from the bottom of the river: *vengeance is over* the words mean. Warplanes fly sideways through the valleys. We wait for one aged psychopath to die. We try to study and to learn. Names of things. One Legend says that Welsh fairies are afraid of iron because the fairies are the lost survivors of a tribe of never-aging children whose ancestors fell victim to a race of conquerors who conquered them with weapons made of iron. *What is the name of that bird? What is ink made of? Could I write in blood? What are words made of?* One time, long ago, I wrote a book about adventures on a desert island. *Isn't that a laugh?* Crusoe used to go around his desert island and, as Orlando did, Crusoe used to carve his name in trees. Crusoe and Orlando were both fictions. They weren't men. Others made them up and wrote them down. Tomorrow, in a book called *The Oxford Companion to the Mind*, I will read an essay titled "Chinese Evidence on the Evolution of Language" so I can learn about the use of pictograms. Tomorrow I will shout at planes and jets that come at us like arrows. Tomorrow I will burn myself on what I take to be a cinder. Tomorrow I will find *the* picture with *the* diagram inside *the* book that tells me finally simply and beyond a doubt the way religion tells some people, *This tiny thing of beauty in the tree outside your window is a chaffinch, Marianne.*

WALES
APRIL 1989

ZELF-PORTRET

JIKES! is that all jou ever think about? *Jourzelf?* I've had it up to *here* with jour zelf-interest, I am bored to tears by jou! *Houp op of ik gil!* Stop this instant or I'll scream. Dutch is so damn weird. I mean: it is a weird weird language. What does *this* mean: *spoorweg*: railroad. What train is this? Whose train of thought? Where am I now? Where are we going? HOLLAND, right. The Low Countries: real low. The Benelux. The nether-lands. Beneath sea level, very nether, territory they call "reclaimed land." We're going Dutch here, darling. We're doing what the Dutch do, dear: DROOGMAKERIJEN: we're making dry.

O for godsake just shut up for once and stop jour crying.

Well GESONDE GEWOONTE jourzelf: here she is in Oostende on her way to Holland on a train, an all-time Low. Is this the Lowest that she's ever been? On land, I mean: I mean

61

is this the lowest that she's ever been on land? Jou bet. The only place that comes to mind to top this Low for lowness is Death Valley back home in the Great Satan but she's never been there. She's been a lot of places, she's had a lot of rides on trains but never to Death Valley, no siree: Look it up in jour home atlas, darling, it's the only entry in the index under "Death," right there between DEASE STRAIT NORTHWEST TERRITORIES CANADA and DEAUVILLE. *Deauville*, now there's a place. She'd seen it in a movie more than twenty years ago: Claude Lelouch, *A Man and a Woman*: fitting movie to remember: fitting title, in her present situache. Yeah: about this movie, why it's fitting, see: there is this guy who is a race car driver and he meets a woman and they fall in love but when they go to a hotel room in (she thinks this is correct:) *Deauville*, the woman gets all overly neurotic with these nightmare visions of her much-loved dear-departed husband so she snaps her bra back on and belts her coat and hops a train for Paris. What happens next is that the race car driver drives his car the length of France from (she thinks this is correct:) *Deauville* to Monte Carlo where he takes part in a car race, turns around and drives all the way to Paris in time to meet the woman on the platform at the *gare* as she gets off the train but of course this feat of driving is impossible and jumbled in her mind and pieces of the plot are obviously missing from her memory but she *is* convinced she's right on these three things: first, there was an awful lot of driving in this movie; second, there was an awful lot of music which went daba daba da throughout the scenes which were about the awful lot of driving; and, third, the director had not told the actress who played the woman who was in love with the race car driver that he, the r.c.d., was going to be there on the platform when she steps down from the train so the expression that's captured on that first-and-only take when she sets eyes on him is actually the real reaction of a real intelligence (the actress's) understanding whatthefuck the movie is about and howthehell it's going to end:

That's what she remembers about this movie called *A Man and a Woman:*

Deauville, and the phenomenon of watching someone seeing something in two ways at once—watching both the actress and the woman she's portraying in the film respond with genuine sincerity from two separate points of view to a single circumstance with a single eloquent expression which translates in several ways:

If I had been that actress, she remembers having thought, *I would have had Lelouch's balls dry-cleaned*, what a bastard, do this, darling, step this way, enter on the stage suspecting nothing so the audience can watch a ton of bricks fall on jou but STAY IN CHARACTER: what's the problem, what do jou mean jou can't remember who jou *are*, just look in any goddam mirror for christsake what are jou, blind?

She is starting to believe she needs to wonder what goes on when a writer/artist tries to make the words/the work of art into a mirror which reflects the writer's/artist's zelf:

The answer's simple, she believes: it turns out mirror-imaged, backwards, baby, imagined the wrong way around, reversed, so fuck it. We all suffer our reversals.

Let's face it, I mean: is this trip The End? It's only Holland, right? And she thinks she's on somekinda goddam pilgrimage or something, right?

Jou bet.

A goodam pilgrim, am I right?

Absolutely. *God*dam pilgrim. In full drab.

Now whatthefuck's she doing?

Standing out in front of Number 263 on the Prinsengracht.

O jesus christ.

And get this, too: it's raining, so she's soaking wet.

Jesus tell her go and smoke some dope or something,

Christ! It's Amsterdam! Tell her go and sportfuck 'til her skin falls off—Some great big Aryan with those Delftblue eyes! Tell her go buy hash! Tell her, christ, they make great chocolate here! Doesn't she like chocolate? Tell her they make beer—great beer! Doesn't she like beer? Does she like to shop? Tell her they make—I don't know—great something, they must make something great, those wooden shoes for christsake, clogs the hell they call them, tulip bulbs or something, *cigars*, sure, what about those what's the kind of Dutch Masters! Tell her she should *lighten up*—!

Too late. She's going in.

She's going in the house?

She's gone.

She's gone into the house?

"The Annex," actually.

I know it's called "The Annex"! *I* read the goddam book! What do jou think? I didn't read the goddam book? We *had* to read the goddam book in those days—

"*Het Achterhuis.*"

I know what the goddam house was called, who do jou think jou're talking to?

"*Das Hinterhaus.*"

I mean, for christsake, what does she think she's doing? She takes a train to Holland so she can visit Anne Frank's *house*? What happened to *fun*? We used to have some *fun*. We used to have, geez, *fun*, she used to be so funny, jou know, she used to be so *warm*, so warm and *real*—

She's going up the stairs.

O *shit*!

These narrow stairs: there is a sign which reads TRAP OP. An arrow pointing UP, so I guess *trap op* is Dutch for—

I know what *trap op* is Dutch for! Get her out of here for christsake call the cops or something—

Now she's standing where the bed once stood.

O geez this is too—

Staring at the pictures on the wall.

. . . masochistic.

Ray Milland.

Can you believe this shit?

Ray Milland. Anne Frank put this picture on her wall of Ray Milland. I mean: star of stage and screen, a Hitchcock type. Straightforward Hitchcock villain.

Listen: next to Hitler any guy looks good . . .

Ray Milland right here next to postcards of Their Little Royal English Highnesses. Margaret and Elizabeth. How old do they look?

Like kids.

And this: a picture of a bowl of strawberries in full color. This: Anne Frank had a picture on her wall of Ginger Rogers. Look at this one: Greta Garbo. This: a picture of a cockatoo. Anne Frank had a picture called *The Lark Song*. Two zelf-portrets, one by Rembrandt, another one by Leonardo, hey: great stuff. A postcard of some monkeys called the, what? *The Chimpanzee Tea Party*—

I think somebody needs to get her outa here—

Hey stop yelling. .

SHE'S IN THE ATTIC!

Hey calm down.

IN THE GODDAM ATTIC, HEAR ME?

What's the matter with—

Why does someone go to Holland just to stand there looking at a goddam *wall*?

Why are jou so—

Why does someone go to all the trouble of a journey just to stand here looking at a goddam photograph of jesus christ I don't believe this *Ray Milland*—?

Well *m'land m'land*, m'lady: thank jour lucky stars for ol' Hieronymous. *Don Bosco*, as they call him in the Prado: Bosch! Hieronymous! The Dutch can really name 'em, can't

they? The Dutch have *names*: Hieronymous, it's like it's
z-o-o-logical or something. Translates to "Jerome" but we
Englishspeaking people can't suppress our little giggles can
we, get real nervous at the way it sounds, horrific-like, I
mean: how'd *jou* like to have a name like his, hey: jou think
jou have problems, how'd jou like to have a name like his *and*
have his vision? Have jou seen his paintings? It's not like she
believes a thing (a man) is nothing but the word which names
him, but: maybe his *name* brought on those holy visions,
have jou ever thought of that? Maybe a thing is nothing *but*
its word, its name, maybe words are *It*, the be-all and the
end-all of man's definition, maybe Bosch was visited by
weirdness because he had a weird name, what do jou think of
that? Born in 's Hertogenbosch, geez, just try and *say* it.
What's the " 's -" stand for? Why is Dutch so deeply nutty?
It's like: maybe Man is not intended to make large-scale rec-
lamations of submerged land. Maybe it leaves water on the
brain and makes weird language out of ordinary things, christ
knows, it makes some weird weird painters. Brueghel (okay,
they were Flemish) but what about van Gogh? They're from
nether-worlds! Rembrandt! *There's* a ray of hope: no weirdy,
he. Vermeer! Van Eyck! Frans Hals! de Kooning! not all of
them were weirdies. Not all of them gave children night-
mares. I mean: most of them were portrait painters, chron-
iclers of wealth, creators of still-lives-with-cheeses, solid
honest burghers in full drab with tonsamoney but that can't
excuse the fact that ol' Hieronymous was Dutch and plenty
weird because of it. Do jou know what they say about him?
That he never traveled outside Holland except maybe for
adventure once or twice he went as far afield as Antwerp.
Talk about jour sun 'n' fun adventure: do jou think he ever
saw a mountain? Maybe being from a Low Country helped
him get a better grasp of Hell, maybe height's connected to
Man's destiny, I mean he was born in 's Hertogenbosch, a
place that's lower than sea level and he spent the whole of his

creation painting devilinfested creepy apocalyptic things
around religious saints who look as if they've watched God
die, so maybe jou should think about it: height. How Low a
something is. In terms of destination. Jou know what a com-
plex thing they say it is. Jou know what they say about
Napoleon:

> *He was so fuckedup about his size he tried to conquer*
> *Russia:*
> *He couldn't tell his squat butt from his elba.*

Are all dictators whackos? Is height the final yardstick of
insanity in rulers? How tall was Attila? Stalin was a giant (so
they say): how tall was Hitler, how Low can the Lowest go,
what final form does evil take? Christ, jou call this a vacation? The next thing that she'll want to do is go and visit
Bergen-Belsen. Babi Yar: hell why stop there, she could keep
on truckin' East, take in all the highspots of annihilation,
shit, Armenia, the Punjab, My Lai and Manchuria, the girl
could start her own real swingin' network of forgotten places
called *Club Dead*, take jou places so forgotten that the crows
don't even fly there anymore. "Listen," she begins to say to
this semiconscious bozo sitting on the train across from her:
Look out the window! What's the matter with jou? Are jou
braindead? Look! Those are wild gladioli growing in the
fields beside the tracks: wild gladioli, man! A fucking
miracle, jou understand? Don't jou understand? They were
going to flood the country! They were going to inundate the
land, the Germans were, when they feared there was a chance
the British might be coming, Anne Frank says so in her
diary, they were going to pull the plug on Holland, *glug*,
consign it to infernal depths, as unreclaimable as History, a
last defense—don't jou think that is a riot, bub? Jou're from
Seattle, geez, the parents paid for jou to come to Europe,
wow, and this is what? jour fifth? jour *sixth* time into Am-

sterdam, no shit, jou must really dig it there, the art, the culture and the people—*what?* O, the sensemilla: O, the weed, the herb: the *grass*: "One will have to try and swim," Anne-at-fourteen wrote in 1944. We shall all put on our bathing suits and caps and swim beneath the water. Nobody will see us. No one will discover we are *j**s*.

Okay okay: let's lighten up, let's tell a little joke.

Let's emulate our rôle model in this disappearance field, let's tell a joke befitting uncle Tom, the doughty Thomas, Pynchon. 'Kay?

Okay.

Pia Zadora.

Poor woman has a joke-quotient equal that of c. dan quayle's but hey let's face it humorists ain't saints, there's no philanthropic mission run by stand-up comics so there she was in Florida, see, Pee. Zed., that diminutive blonde bombshell herzelf, playing the leading rôle of A., her other-zelf, A. Frankly, in *The Diary of Anne Frank* and playing it, jou guessed it, like *an ingénue* in a Miami Beach supper club. Up goes the curtain, if there was one, on the Second Act and when the actors playing Nazi*momzers* came on stage and started sniffing 'round the secret hiding place, some *tzaddik* from Miami Shores who was winding up his five-course meal of calves' foot jelly, Turkey Maryland, sweet and sour kneidlan and potato kugel with some sour cream and strudel hollers out with everyone's approval, "Schmucks, SHE'S IN THE ATTIC!"

Poor Zed-ora: can't go anywhere without some joke, but hey: remember Shelley Winters in the movie of *The Diary of?* Remember how she played the rôle of poor Mrs. Van Daan?

Bloozy, baby, right ol' Winters part, pouty, frowsty, petulant, bedizened.

"Too many vegetables in the evening makes her consti-pated," Anne wrote about the real Mrs. V.D.

Anne was always writing about her.

Woman's *dead* for christsake, died in Auschwitz with her husband but the last conversation Anne recorded between the two of them goes like this:

> *Mr. Van Daan* (standing up): "It's about time you shut your mouth. One day I'll show you that I'm right; sooner or later you'll get enough of it. I can't bear any more of your grousing. You're so infuriating but you'll stew in your own juice one day."

Six weeks before they were betrayed to the Dutch Nazis, Anne sketched this final portrait of her: "Mrs. Van Daan is desperate, talks about a bullet through her head, prison, hanging, and suicide . . . She's offended that Dussel doesn't enter into her flirtations with him, as she'd hoped, afraid that her husband is smoking all the fur-coat money away, she quarrels, uses abusive language, cries, pities herself, laughs and then starts a fresh quarrel again. What on earth can one do with such a foolish, blubbering specimen?"

Saturday, 11th July, 1942:

Anne writes: "I expect you will be interested to hear what it feels like to 'disappear'; well, all I can say is that I don't know myself yet . . . it is more like being on holiday in a very peculiar boarding-house . . . Our little room looked very bare at first with nothing on the wall; but thanks to Daddy who had brought my film-star collection and picture postcards on beforehand, and with the aid of paste-pot and brush, I have transformed the wall into one gigantic picture."

• • •

So I stand there where Anne must have stood and I look out the window as she must have done and I wonder about *por-tret*sure, about por-trayal/*be*-trayal, about landscapes and ghosts, the artist's/writer's lies, about fugitive zelves, about history and tyrants and all that's fleeting: she had a mustache. What breaks the heart in the end are the facts, not the fiction: Mandela's release, the actual seeing-of-him that first time on TV as he walked, gray-haired gimp-gaited man, out of the portrait we had fixed him in. Fact cracks the heart the way no story can so jou go in search of facts, to see this wall Anne made into a giant "picture." In the end it moves jou but misleads jou. Have jou ever shaved a person's head? I had to do it once—*she*, the woman in this tale, not *I*—she didn't *have* to do it, no, she helped her husband do it as a form of a disguise. When we told his sister what I'd done his sister shouted eeeeek although she couldn't see him so when I went to Amsterdam and stood before the picture wall trying to imagine Anne I thought about her hair I thought about the pictures that I'd seen of prisoners in the deathcamps with shaved heads and I remembered that she'd written in this room about her hair, about her mustache, age fourteen:

> . . . *I give myself a thorough wash and general toilet; it occasionally happens (only in the hot weeks or months) that there's a tiny flea floating in the water. Then teeth cleaning, hair curling, manicure, and my cotton-wool pads soaked in hydrogen peroxide (to bleach black moustache hairs)*

The Nazis shaved her head at Auschwitz, shaved her sister's, mother's, father's, boyfriend's, boyfriend's parents'; shaved their pubic hairs but numbers numb, a heart cracks open once, with a specific. Then it closes 'round that grain, embeds it, opens, closes, opens for another, hides its circumstantial secrets; dies.

Stories come like storms, they come like weather or like natural disasters. Something happens and jou think: a noise. Something chinks against the armor and jou lift the lid a little, wonder: whatthefuck's the clatter: It's like listening to Dutch.

So here she is in Amsterdam where there isn't any *amerikaanse uitspraak.*

When she disembarks at Centraal Station from Oostende her name is on the front page of all the English papers, some misinterpretation of her private life is squeezed inside a blackedged box page one herald tribune and why, I wonder, is she always watching moments of dividedzelf in *goddam* european *goddam* train *goddam them* stations?

STAY IN CHARACTER! she tells herzelf, don't slip don't skip a beat don't beat retreat don't slide elusive from the frame re-main re-mand re-medial rem-brandt: hey talk about some REMs here, cuddles, talk about some Rapid-I-Moves she would love to wake from this one but she goes to her hotel and switches on some Dutch TV and guess what's there, Dr. Kildare and Toshiro Mifune in a made-for-television (whatthefuck is *not* these days?) movie-of-the-book called *Shogun* and Kildare's talkin' English which is fine with her because that's *one* language she still thinks she can understand but Mifune's speaking Japanese.

So her eyes because they're trained to do so move across the subtitles um hmmm but then a strange thing happens.

Kildare speaks in English and there are still subtitles on the screen.

Not until The News come on does she clue in she's sitting beneath sea level thinking that she's translating Japanese into *amerikaanse* by reading words on screen in Dutch.

She can't read Dutch.

I mean: can jou? Who can? It's too entirely weird. They put this thing, this thing this

z.o.z.

on the bottom of a page like everybody and her mother oughta know that zee. o. zed. is Dutch-in-short for *zie ommezijde*, meaning something close to p.t.o. or flip it, bub.

> Roll over.
> Turn the page.
> Carry on.
> *Please continue.*
> Zee o zee.

It's like I've never seen a language with so many *zee* words in it in my life. *Zee*ziek, *zee*man, *zee*meermin. *Zee* is Dutch for *sea* and they like to drop one into places every chance they get so there she is reading down a list of things

306.	FRANK	MARGOT	16.2.26
307.	FRANK	OTTO	12.5.89
308.	FRANK	EDITH	16.1.00
309.	FRANK	ANNELIESE	12.6.29

and she comes to *z.o.z.* dropped in there at the bottom of the page and she's supposed to know there is a future, more to come, to be continued. It's cute-looking really when jou think about it (as far as abbrevs. go) becauze jou can read it backwardzupzidedown and itz ztill the zame way all the way around.

Now try this experiment: go stand on the Prinsengracht across from Anne Frank's House and stare into the water of the Prince Canal.

Can jou see the House reflected?

Great.

Two houses, huh.

Which house is real?

The one reflected on the water or the one that's built on reclaimed land?

Which house is hidden from the other?

Which house hid Anne who hid her diary?

The thing jou have to understand is this:

The list of possibilities is endless and the writer always lies.

Someone turned the Franks, the hidden, in. Someone, a good neighbor a stout burgher in full drab traded information for a what? an extra ration? free passage on the tram? the zelf-dizolving fantazy that he-or-she could live a little longer, live a little freer of hiz-or-her own fears?

Fear floods the listless place the way the *zee* floods over nether lands so pay attention stay alert, betrayal is an act in trade, discovery can result in being sent away or being sent to death:

Build might-y picture walls around the zelf, make lists:

The lists are endless:

There's a list of all the zelf-words in the Berlitz *engels-nederlands* woordenboek including *zelfstrijkend* which means drip-dry and *zelfmoord*, word for suicide.

There's a list of all the zelf-portrets that Rembrandt painted:

Bareheaded, 1629
1631
1632
with Saskia, 1635
with Saskia, 1636
1640
1652
1657

1658
as St. Paul, 1661
holding his Palette, Brushes & Maulstick, 1663
Laughing, 1668
1669

In all of them he has a mustache.

There's a list of places, towns I meant to visit to see picture walls, names of towns which have museums where the works of Bosch are housed: Vienna – Rotterdam – New York – Madrid – Berlin – New Haven – Venice – Washington – Lisbon – Frankfurt – Ghent – Paris – Munich – Philadelphia:

His paintings are more places than he ever was.

There's a list of things Bosch painted:

The Seven Deadly Sins
The Four Last Things

There's a list of numbers on the page entitled JUDEN-TRANSPORT AUS DEN NIEDERLANDEN–LAGERWERTERBORK from number 301

ENGERS ISIDOR 30.4.93

to number 350

GOLDBERG HANS 5.6.10

in which four FRANKS are listed as being transported out of Amsterdam to the camp the week before the British landed—then some GELDERS, GINSBERGS, a GLOWINSKI-STREEP. One Sara. A Henry. Sadok. Max. Fanny. Israel. Isaac. Klara. Kalman.

So where does it exist, our history, in these lists?

Where does the past exist?

It lies submerged, it lies in lies, a land that's disappearing even as it happens, lost to reclamation.

Zie ommezijde, continue, please, what have I forgotten to write down?

The birds, that's right, the birds, a woman that I met in Bruxelles told me this, a woman who survived the camp at Bergen-Belsen where Anne died talked to me about the birds outside the camp, the songbirds, described them as a *leitmotif* so there jou are, transfixed by the specific, stopped dead on jour own tracks, jour heart cracked open to receive what she said next:

We could see the birds outside. We could hear them.

Inside there was nothing that resembled life.

Nothing looked like anything we knew.

It was the end of everything.

We thought, who knows? Something wrong with the locale.

Something in the water or the air. Something which kills people but not birds.

Some fatal something in the food supply perhaps.

We didn't know.

Few, only, knew it was SS.

We couldn't think that it was people who were doing this to us.

We thought it was a natural disaster.

So jou take the train, jou paint a portrait, write a fiction, read the papers, misremember movies, fantasize some conversations, note the landscape, plagiarize, cross channels, watch TV and tell another lie: there are six million ways to die at least, six million ways the zelf can end, the *zee*, the final letter in one's alphabet, the big *omega*, *zed*, the zee-omega-zed of the zelf so here we are in nether lands where everything lies, hidden, and everything that isn't hidden lies, reflected, up-sidedown, beginning from that line, exactly, where it touches on the other's surface, where it touches at another zelf, so please help me out. What are we supposed to do, my friend, what the hell are we supposed to do. Jou talk now. I'm invisible. Jou tell me how we end. Jou're the artist. I'm just the artist's friend.

z.o.z.

LONDON
FEBRUARY 1990

ESO ES

A bird is an instrument working according to mathematical law.

Accordingly we may say that such an instrument fabricated by man lacks nothing but the soul of man.

—LEONARDO DA VINCI

FIFTY-SEVEN YEARS AGO while hunting quails several miles from Zaragoza, the former occupant of No. 7 Plaza de Justicia third floor corner rooms had shot a Spanish angel of undetermined sex and killed it and since Time is that one thing which stops all other things from happening at once and since Angels have no use for Time the first demand for retribution, a deaththreat so to speak, the Angels' vengeance, one Angel-killer's life (would the killer, then, become an Angel?) in exchange for the Exterminated One, arrived at No. 7 third floor corner rooms half-a-century-and-a-few-years-late one Friday morning in October, and it came by telephone.

Godless cutthroat angelslayer, the caller's voice informed the current occupant, *Prepare to meet your Doom.*

The voice which spoke these words did not identify itself. It was a sweet celestial voice, incorporeal. It spoke in English with a Spanish accent but the occupant—he is known to those who know him, as Modesto—does not understand the English language. *Qué?* he shouts—*Eso—? Es?*

Even as he stands there shouting Modesto knows the telephone hasn't functioned ever since the excavation at La Seo had begun eleven years ago and furthermore he knows the telephone has never, shall we say, really functioned even prior to the excavation and, moreover, on this particular Friday morning the telephone has not what one could characterize as having really *rung*.

What the telephone has done is signal.

It has signaled to Modesto.

It has summoned him to come in from the balcony where he is standing by the birdcage with a bag of millet in his hand, feeding his two lovebirds, El Niño and Encarnación. The telephone has signaled thus: three shorts, three longs, three shorts again—a sort of drumming on his rib cage from within, a sort of hopskip and a jump-jump in his heart. The telephone had not exactly rung, because it couldn't. Nevertheless a breathy childvoice had spoken eight words in English with a Spanish accent into Modesto's ear while he stood shouting in the third floor corner room before he scratched his head and put the phone down, rolled a globe of millet on his tongue and wondered if the candle he had purchased at Nostra Señora del Pilar had been snuffed by some exterminating blast before the prayer that he had paid for—*Save me, Mother, from women seeking husbands and save me from the Evil Eye and save me, too, from Unemployment so that two birds will have enough to eat to raise their songs to You in Heaven, by Your Good Grace*—before the candle he had paid for had its wicked chance to raise his wishes as a signal up to Heaven.

Who was up there anyway? Modesto often wondered. Was anyThing or anyBody even watching? Birds, Modesto knew, were up there. But Higher-up than birds Modesto's brainwork couldn't soar. His was not a willing certainty to trust in things he couldn't see. He couldn't see the sense of learning, for example: history. Physics: He couldn't see the kernel of a reason in the quest to crack the atom or to unify the fields in fact he didn't even know that men existed who had given their accumulated lives to scientific postulations which attempt to prove the Universe is something draped around Mankind in order to be understood and finally, finitely, defined. He was not a very modern man, Modesto. He didn't know (how could he *not?*) a single word in any other language than his own maternal Spanish, even after years of sitting through those weekly Masses in the Vulgate, and even though he knew about *el bomb,* the Mushroom Cloud, *El Matador,* he was entirely unformed on the subject of *aborto.* Not a very modern man at all, Modesto: nor was he religious. If there was someThing Higher-up-than-birds, a someThing Catholic, for instance, then under that Thing's scrutiny Modesto didn't shine. Under that Thing's scrutiny Modesto was a dull speck in the sequined fabric of believers, an unfused stick inside a box of firecrackers; a dud. Unlike most men of Zaragoza he didn't have a sister cousin uncle brother nephew in the cloth, nor had he suffered under nuns, so he responded to religious practice with the same confusion that a timid man evinces every time he meets a stranger. Modesto is a man who lives in fear of meeting strangers. His is a soul which shies from crossing signals, he's a man who will proceed at peril of getting lost down streets he doesn't know instead of being made a captive to a stoplight on a curb beside a stranger. He never rides the bus, he never goes to places he can't walk to: he is a man who lives in fear of someone coming up to him to raise a modern, unforeseen abstraction.

This is who Modesto is: a shy man who loves birds.

This is what Modesto looks like: unfeathered, wingless; unassuming.

This is what Modesto thinks: A person shouldn't yell into a telephone that hasn't rung.

A person ought to be a man, for once.

A person ought to make an effort to complain.

About the fireworks.

The fireworks were threatening to kill the birds.

Not only his own heart's delights, not only proud El Niño and Encarnación, no, he was not a selfish man, his interests were not those of self-: the fireworks were threatening the city's birds, the whole ornitho-population of his hometown Zaragoza. Swallows nestlings fledglings swifts doves pigeons to say nothing of the crows and martins had no resting place beneath the fireworks at night, they swooped down streets halfcrazy dropping shit like milky tears and he, Modesto, was fed up. *Oké,* he says aloud to no one in the silence after the telephone has signaled, *the time has come for me to act.*

He doesn't know his life has just been threatened.

He doesn't know he is about to die—*who does?*

He doesn't know that someThing up there doesn't understand the signals, still he thinks the time has come for him to act.

He doesn't know the sky is falling, so he goes to have his shoes shined as a sign of his intentions.

Don't imagine they are anything but of the cheapest leather.

Don't imagine they are anything but black.

That Modesto goes to have his shoes shined at this moment is significant because no sooner has he turned into Calle de Prudencio to avoid a crossing signal, than he's halted halfway down the block by an approaching blind man, white stick sweeping 'cross the pavement like a turret gun, and as Modesto steps aside to let him pass and presses his thin frame against the whitewashed wall beneath its wooden eaves a splat of birdmerde hits his shoe. As he sees it land, looking like a bit of spinach in a buttery stew, he, being Modesto, thinks the only thing the least bit curious about the incident is that he hasn't seen a blind man in this street for years, but the question that we have to ask before we understand what happens next is, *Is it possible that angels die?* The answer is, it's possible for Spanish angels. Not that angels carry passports, they don't need them.

But dying once is easy.

Dying once in Spain is commonplace.

Dying twice is something that's reserved for Spanish angels.

Soon there is another detour on the route Modesto takes:

In Calle de la Manifestación he encounters a flock of parrots dressed like priests—(it's that time of year, October, when priests wear feather green)—so he backtracks to the street which runs along the Roman Wall beside the Central Market and, ducking into that, intending to buy mushrooms from the banks along the Ebro, fresh with knobs of humus clinging to them, he is delivered before gamebirds hanging by their throats, squabs and partridges trussed up by their little legs on ribbons cheek to jowl like puppets next to ducks and rabbits, necks of geese looped like firehoses with eyes still bright as morning stars—Even in a city as sanctified and holy as his Zaragoza, there are sights too brutal to be seen, sometimes, by people like Modesto, people like himself who have to seek asylum in the market at this time of year from priests parading through the streets as parrots or from strangers or to look for mushrooms on the way, circuitous, albeit, for a shoeshine which, owing to the route he'd taken to avoid the stoplight and the blind man, he now socially-acceptably most definitely required because a bird had *shat* on one of them but then in front of Señora Setelo's bacalao and olive stand Modesto runs into a son of Uncle I-I's.

Or rather: a son of Uncle I-I's runs into Modesto and a piece of bacalao like sandstone shatters on the ground from underneath the boy's thin shirt.

The boy bends down, picks up the goods and disappears into the market crowd.

Thief! Modesto hears Señora Setelo call. In an age of peaches here's a youth purloining salt cod, boy of ancient tastes, Modesto thinks, but Uncle I-I is a man of influence, an eye doctor now given to the authorship of tourist guides to Zaragoza, he has peered into the eyes of half the population of the city so he knows their souls and now his son, this boy—what was he called? Fatso—? No, no, *gordo,* Fat Boy—this overfed cherubic youth why is *he* stealing food, his father isn't poor and he is not exactly underweight, but then a stranger standing by the *chorizo* and *salchichon* stall says to Modesto Kids today. They steal for fun.

The stranger seems to think an answer might develop from the agitation his remark engenders in Modesto but little does he know about real panic so he thinks Modesto might be suffering—who knows?—a heart attack as he backs himself into a wall of eggplants out of fear. Then a marching band appears around a cart of melons and Modesto cannot catch his breath. A bass drum booms, the trumpet blares and birds high in the rafters start to flap their wings and swoop amid the dust raised from the spider webs and nests and, fed by wisps of raffia around the apples and the oranges and the melons and the figs and tangerines, combining with a cloud of sawdust rising from the butchers' stalls, a celestial smaze descends, obscuring strangers and their produce from whom and which there flies one man, almost invisible, not stopping to observe the beauty of the shapes of all of nature's mushrooms.

"I tell you," he tells Paco later while his shoes are being shined, "I can't figure out this world."

"The world is nuts," Paco puts forth as an explanation.

It is Paco's only answer to a customer's lament and he always speaks it toward their shoes.

"Today," Modesto says, "you won't believe it but you know there is a telephone in the rooms I rent? It rang."

"It didn't."

"No."

"It didn't?"

"It didn't but it did. The telephone."

"Forgive me, but. The world is nuts."

"It's disconnected."

"Like the nuts. The phone is not connected. Do nuts not fall and disconnect from trees?"

"It rang. The telephone. Nuts ring?"

"What I'm saying like I always say is: The world? Is nuts. I'm not saying: World? She's a disconnected phone. The world she's not a disconnected telephone. But now you mention it: perhaps."

"Then what happens? Someone tells me something I don't know. That's when I saw dots."

"We all see dots. I get them bending over shoes sometimes."

"And dashes, too. Before my eyes. Just like hot air balloons."

"You should have your eyes examined."

"Perhaps like bubbles, says it better. Floating."

"Go see Uncle I-I."

"Like bubbles in my soul. Perhaps the soul is fizzy what you call it, *con gas*."

"Try to see him before lunch."

"Perhaps the soul is carbonated."

"As far as I'm concerned the sole's a callus. Piece of leather. What's this shit you got here on this shoe?"

"Pigeon shit."

"How come you're wearing it on top?"

"Where should a person wear pigeon shit? Beneath?"

"It ruins shoes."

"Shoes are made to ruin."

"I like shoes. You like these birds too much."

"I *am* a bird."

"And I'm a *millonario.*"

"That's what I'm going to tell the people at the City Hall."

"That I'm a *millonario?*"

"That I'm a bird. I think and feel like birds and something must be done about the fireworks. I plan to be persuasive."

"In these shoes?"

"You'll see. The time has come."

"The men at City Hall will shit on shoes like these. You need new shoes. Forget the City Hall. Go see Uncle I–I. He can fix whatever fireworks you want. Some big message in the sky? HEY SEXY BABY BOFF ME 'TIL MY NUTS FALL OFF—"

"*Again* with falling nuts?"

"Big message in the sky—anything you want. Uncle I–I can arrange it. Fireworks? All it takes is money. More than you possess, though, judging from these shoes."

"It must be stopped!"

"The poverty?"

"The fireworks!"

"You want to stop the fireworks?"

"They're bothering the birds!"

"Birdbrain: it's Festival. *Pilar.* People like some pyrotechnics."

"People aren't the only beings on this planet!"

"You need to have your eyes examined. Then your head. Go see Uncle I–I."

"First I'll go to City Hall."

"Where they'll shit on you."

"Higher things have shat on me."

"What you know from shit could fill a bubble in your

soul, Modesto. You don't even know that things that shit shit worse the more the things that shit have legs."

Modesto blinks.

Dots—(in threes)—and Dashes—(ditto)—float before his eyes.

"*Qué*?" he whispers.

Paco gestures. "The only thing whose shit stinks worse than politicians' is a camel. Or possibly an elephant." He spits, professionally, at Modesto's shoes. "You like opera? You should see *Aida*. You should see what animals will do on center stage. The elephant. *Piuùi*."

But Modesto isn't listening.

Somewhere there is someThing that is sending him a signal.

English—as a language—was not the first of pleasures on fat I-I's tongue. The first was chocolate; the second one was cream. The third was Spanish—(as it's spoken in Castile)— the fourth, paella. Uncle I-I was a glutton for paella, but English was a little further down the list of things that made his mouth feel happy. It was No. 35. Nevertheless whenever he encountered it, just as whenever he encountered sheep brains on a menu, he always tried it with great relish because his memory convinced him that he liked it better than he really did. Once he had eaten sheep brains cooked with butter and some wheat germ and paprika and ever since, each time he saw the item listed on a menu, he would order it and eat it and be disappointed. Several hundred times sheep brains had disappointed him against that one time he remembered yet: his memory was unaffected. Same with English. Once, a half a life ago, he'd learned to speak the language in ten days when two Americans had come to Zaragoza in his cousin's limousine from Bilbao on their way to Barcelona, Alicante,

Toledo and Madrid, when his cousin fell victim to *el coñac* and to save the family honor and the German car they had all at one time or another contributed their earnings to, Uncle I-I took the driver's seat and drove as fast as he learned English. It was not a wasted journey. In Valencia he found Hortènsia—(an angel-genius with paella)—and after driving for ten days he sold the Mercedes in Madrid and paid the members of his family back with interest what they'd loaned their good-for-nothing alcoholic relative, then he used the proceeds to enroll himself in eyesight school and send for Hortense from Valencia to come and make paella for him, as his wife. His English he let simmer for some decades 'til he served it up again as good as new, to launch his guidebook business. *In the XIXth century,* Uncle I-I's English language guide to Zaragoza starts, *the city was immolated by the most heroic gest in humankind.*

You can buy this book at any kiosk.

The present day Zaragoza, it continues, "is erected on the site once occupied by the roman city Caesaraugusta only remembered through numismatic vestiges left traversed by the iberian rider. I invite you, visiting friend, to stroll a autumn night of Zaragoza through the district near La Seo. You may make wise remarks on the appearing none of monumental buildings but I shall show you a touristic fun the vigorous evocative of which will leave you gasping when you startle this unique islamic catholic mosque cathedral."

Eat! Uncle I-I startles at Modesto when Modesto sits down at his table gasping somewhat at the vigorous evocative of only a starched napkin placed before him where a plate of food should be. "Hunger often causes dots before one's eyes," the great man says. "Very nearly always hunger, dots, except with women in their *menopausia.* Sun, too, will do it. You were standing in the sun? You look a little pinked."

Modesto searches for a way to hide the flushed embarrassment arriving, rosy, to his face as soon as Uncle I-I speaks the words *la menopausia* at table—(especially in front of children!)—but, also, at the same time, he searches for a knife and fork, a plate, some food. Around the table: Modesto, searching, plate-less, fork-less, knife-less, speechless; Agnès, one of Uncle I-I's leftover mothers-in-law; Uncle I-I and Uncle I-I's three unlikely sons. There are four plates, only, on the table. Agnès, it appears, is only there to serve and watch. And Modesto, after all, is uninvited.

"A place setting for Modesto!" Uncle I-I, ever sympathetic, shouts; and Agnès, wheezing, brings a saucer. "Silver!" Uncle I-I bellows. Agnès lays a butter knife. "See what misery besets me!" Uncle I-I pines. Still, they wait for food. His sons, staring toward the center of the table, poise themselves with horizontal forks and upright knives, at ready. "Beloved Montserrat has left me," I-I laments.

"Ah," Modesto manages to murmur. There is some confusion in his mind, aggravated by the placement of the butter knife and saucer, as to whom, exactly, "beloved Montserrat" has been in Uncle I-I's life. For a panicked moment, Modesto toys with the idea that perhaps "beloved Montserrat" was Uncle I-I's cat. Modesto is afraid of cats. Or perhaps "beloved Montserrat" was Uncle I-I's partner in the guidebook business. Then, fixing on the youngest of the different sons, Modesto suffers total recall at the likeness of the boy to his maternal parent and remembers that the "Montserrat" in question had been Uncle I-I's third, most recent wife.

"Can it be?" Modesto asks. "*Three* wives have left?"

"Things come in threes," the *maestro* tells him, pointing with his fork around the table at his sons.

"But lovebirds come in pairs," Modesto says.

The food arrives.

"You see," Modesto says. He watches how the children watch the food. "In twos," he adds.

But no one's heard. What materializes from the kitchen has taken everybody's breath away.

To begin with, bread; three loaves—a dense dark one asparkle with salt crystals, a cloche-shaped sweetly fragrant brioche, and a round of olive bread.

Then there is a dish of honey; one of butter; one of almonds, one of dates.

There is a plate of mashed potatoes shaped in squares and fried in oil with anchovies, served with mayonnaise and capers.

There is roast chicken.

There are long pork sausages, and snails.

There is an illustrated salad.

There are *calamares, huevos duros, jamón, ostras, rábanos, sardinas.*

And then there is paella.

Three paellas: one for each of Uncle I-I's wives. A *paella valenciana*—chicken, shrimps, prawns, mussels, squid, peas, chili, pepper, garlic, in honor of Hortènsia, his Catholic wife. *Paella moruna*—lamb, chickpeas, saffron, okra and sultanas, in honor of Maryam, his Arab wife. *Paella cubana* with bananas and fried egg, in honor of "beloved Montserrat," the Jewess who had only recently abandoned him.

The children of these women eye the food.

Perched across from them, the solitary diner on the other side, Modesto catches their crossfire kicks beneath the table and he draws his feet up on the chair-rung like a bird and incidentally folds his hands across his lap, protectively.

Uncle I-I lifts his hand—it holds a silver fork—and says, *Let's pray.*

Our father, Uncle I-I starts.

He hesitates.

"Close your eyes, Modesto," he instructs.

Modesto screws his eyes shut then what follows is the longest prayer he's ever heard, during which his gastric juices chorus like impatient offstage ghosts. He thinks about the bread beneath his nose. His right hand, like a vine sent shooting by his stomach, snakes up from his lap and starts by inches past his saucer toward a single crumb. Fighting off his hunger, he forms a fist, convinced that soon the word *A-men* will dawn and whole crusts, honey, fruits, the juice of plum tomatoes, broths, will be his own. In the dark of his frustration he sees spots. He envisions yolks. He is too artless to envision praying for the end of Uncle I-I's prayer, but still a small petition starts to form from his creative side: *Holy Mother, by Your Grace, bless my uncle with some brevity.* The next thing that he knows he hears the word *A-men* and he opens up one eye to see if he has dreamed it.

Then Modesto opens both his eyes.

His mouth, not to be forgotten, falls open, too.

What he sees, he can't believe.

The serving plates are empty.

Modesto blinks.

"*Eso es,*" his uncle says. A bit of something green is caught between his two front teeth. "You must come again sometime," he says. "And you must come again next Friday for an eye appointment."

Uncle I-I belches.

"Fridays are reserved," he says. "I don't see many people from the public anymore."

His voice sounds deeper.

"Fridays are reserved for those I see."

Uncle I-I smiles.

"After all, you're family," Uncle I-I tells Modesto.

Modesto feels confused. He feels like he's been sleeping. He can't remember *how* they are related—how *he*, Modesto, is related to this man. Was he his mother's brother? Was his father married to his sister? The only thing Modesto can remember is that Uncle I-I always *was*, right from the beginning, he was always *there*, the fat man in the linen suit who searched the eyes of people with diminished sight and saw their souls, professionally.

"But," Modesto stammers—(*it's as though he has acquired second sight!*): "Friday is too late."

Uncle I-I eyes him.

He starts to pick his teeth.

By this time, too, his sons are restless.

"I assure you, nephew," Uncle I-I says, "there's no hurry. No one dies from spots before the eyes. Except bus drivers. Forgive me, but: you drive a bus?"

The sons of Uncle I-I start to try to kill each other with their knives and forks.

"I mean," Modesto says, alarmed about his safety, "next Friday is too late to stop the fireworks."

The sons of Uncle I-I fall upon each other on the floor. There are muffled accusations of conspiracy and theft.

The good names of their mothers are invoked. Religions, three religions, are profaned, religiously.

"*The*—?" Uncle I-I cocks his head as if he's deaf.

"*Fireworks*," Modesto emphasizes. "The fireworks are threatening the birds."

Uncle I-I stares at him.

"Next Friday is too late," Modesto says. "Something terrible will happen to the birds by then."

Modesto wants to put his hands up to his ears.

He hesitates. Do birds have ears?

He thinks perhaps he understands Beethoven:

"They'll die," he says.

"The birds," he says.

"The *birds*," Modesto gestures.

From his mouth his uncle draws a much-sucked bone, a chicken wing, and holds it.

He throws it to his sons.

"There is nothing I can do," he says.

The boys are tearing at each other.

"Fireworks," he says.

He licks his fingers:

"People want them."

Friday prayers, Modesto realizes he is thinking. Why is he thinking that? What's a Friday prayer? A prayer said on a Friday? For a Friday? *Today* is Friday! he realizes. Unholy day! Day of the week Ourlordandsaviourjesuschrist was sacrificed: *Holy Mother, I am hungry. I am hungry for the first time in my life.* I have never been so hungry, Modesto starts to realize. Should I pray for food? What is suitable to pray for? If only I were better trained in things pertaining to the soul! He thinks: To pray for food, is that permitted? I'm not really starving after all, there's bread at home, a half a loaf, *manchego* in a cheesecloth on the window sill, a jar of cherries in dark syrup on the shelf. Could I pray to end the fireworks? Could I pray to end a life? What had Uncle I-I prayed for when he prayed? For love? For food? For Montserrat? Where had all the food gone? With the wives? Where had all the wives gone? Down his gullet? *Basta!* I must not allow myself such thoughts! I'm seeing spots again, from hunger there's no doubting, Uncle I-I hit the problem on its head: I must have something to eat. I'll go to El Tubo *eeiyy* I feel so empty in the head my head is floating: Have I money with me? You could knock me over. Here, sit down:

Modesto sits on what he thinks is a stone bench but which is actually a low stone drinking trough, now dry, for animals. It's lined with tin beneath its curved stone lip. At one end there's a stone head of an angel, its mouth open, through which the drinking water used to flow. The trough is in the street in front of Uncle I-I's house. There is excavation work nearby. Uncle I-I's three unlikely sons are running through the rubble exploding bricks on one another. They are making world war three. *Enough!* Modesto thinks of shouting at them but he has no strength. He wishes he could lift away just simply lift, like prayer. Enough! what are you killing one another for?

"Tell me please?" he is aware of someone whispering near him: "What the signals mean?"

Modesto jumps, afraid of contact with a stranger and *eeiyy!* he has to hold onto his hat to keep his head from taking to the heavens, has there ever been a head as aerial as his?

"The signals?" he's aware of someone saying. "Every night. This week. The meaning?"

Modesto tries to verify the source of this inquiry so he can run from it but when he looks around the only souls in sight are those three in the rubble kicking up a rumpus.

"*Las señals,*" he hears someone saying. "After dark. *Significa qué . . . ?*"

Modesto looks into the trough.

Bubbles are escaping from the mouth of the stone angel.

Bubbles fill the tin-lined drinking place.

Bubbles—one! two! three!—pursue him toward El Tubo.

Visiting Friend! the sacred text of Uncle I-I's tells its reader,

Zaragoza offers you without walls the embrace of its nobile hospitality, its mudejar liths, its Market and odd niches, its peaceful river Ebro receiving with affection into its great gulf the streams from different mountain ranges, its restfulness of squares, its charms of parks and more its turbulating life and its surprises of 'El Tubo' full of air impregnated with insist of many gastronomic aromas. Come nearer and be welcome, traveller friend. Have a rest in this Most Nobile, Most Loyal, Most Heroic, Always Heroic, Very Hospitable and Immortal City of Zaragoza but remember:

QUIEN VISITA ZARAGOZA // He who visits Zaragoza

Y NO VA A VER 'EL TUBO' // And doesn't go to see 'El
Tubo'
BIEN PUEDE DECIR // Can rightly say
QUE EN ZARAGOZA NO ESTUVO // He hasn't been to
Zaragoza.

If, in the middle of an open road between two towns on what
has been for miles an entirely untrafficked and untraveled
byway, there suddenly appears a traffic jam of colossal pro-
portions the complexity and duration of which exists outside
the realm of physics, then that open road's a *Spanish* road and
every Spanish road leads either to Franco's mausoleum or to
a Spanish city and in every Spanish city there are people so
accustomed to dramatic intervention of the chaos which
arises out of nothing every day and *honks!* and *argues!* lasts an
hour and then goes away that they wouldn't think it strange
if angels started falling from the sky, directing traffic.

Fortunately for them, and for the planet, Modesto
doesn't drive.

Fortunately for him if angels started falling from the sky
he would mistake them all for birds and although he didn't
know it, his life had now become a consequence of all such
previous mistakes. One mistake after another had com-
pounded to his sum like pesetas earning negligible interest
held in trust. He should have listened to his mother, followed
in his father's footsteps and married young but other people
frightened him, his father frightened him, so did his mother,
so, sometimes, did his own reflection in a mirror, so there
was no use thinking he would ever go too near a woman, no,
although once a year he did press his lips against the glass in
the cathedral behind which stood the statue of the Virgin on
her pillar but that was different because it was behind glass
and because it was a statue not a real woman and even if it had
been a real woman it would have been the Virgin, so. That
was different. That was veneration. That was something that

he had to do because he lived in Zaragoza. If he lived in Santiago de Compostela for example then he wouldn't kiss a glass in a cathedral once a year he'd wear a cockleshell and venerate the relics of St. James but that was Santiago de Compostela and this was Zaragoza on the Ebro in the middle of Aragon and everybody knew the Virgin visited St. James here in-the-flesh on 2 January 40 A.D. and handed him the pillar of faith *el pilar* on which she's standing still, jewel-encrusted, behind the glass, even though she would have been over one hundred years old and even though there's no proof St. James ever came to Spain even though the Spanish say his bones are buried there.

Another thing Modesto should have done was stay away from birds.

The birds were clearly a mistake.

His downfall, so to speak.

And he should have never taken Paco's advice and wasted time with Uncle I-I, he should have gone directly to the real *patróns* at City Hall and all this business with the fireworks would be behind him now instead of nagging at him with his hunger. He'd have a bite to eat, hot chocolate and a plain cheese sandwich, and get on with it, he thought, but cars are not permitted in El Tubo and the streets, such as they are, are narrow winding sidewalks lined with *tapas* bars and packed with people, strangers, a disaster of them like a traffic jam, hundreds, thousands, milling, pilgrims to the festival of *El Pilar,* men and women, children, dressed in red and black the colors of Aragon *looking like turkeys:*

Modesto takes off.

What do people *want?* he wonders. Is it true, as Uncle I-I says, that people want these fireworks? Things that make their babies cry? So much of this city is now falling down why can't anything be fixed? Look at this: an edifice of broken windows: dust as permanent as soil: *cerrado por obras /* closed for works / bridge *en restauración,* desultory excavation for a yellowed crumbling Roman wall, *les rogamos dispensen las molestias /* we hope we haven't caused you any trouble. Well you have! Modesto wants to tell someone in charge of all the rubble: *lots!* just take a look at what this mess has done to someone's shoes:

His shoes are once again despicable. *Twice* in one day, what a business. All this excavation in the forecourt of La Seo—what do they expect to find? a Spanish treasure? no one digs in Spain for Spanish gold. No, the cathedral of La Seo, facing City Hall at a right angle, was built eight centuries ago over the remains of an old mosque. What are they digging up? Old ruins. What does it do to shoes? It shits on them. Feet are not made for walking through the mess that History provides, Modesto's black shoes have discovered. He wishes that he had no feet for where he wants to go: and where is that? Some place where shoes do not exist. Black shoes are the lowest of the low of man's inventions. Why do I waste time cleaning up these shoes? Modesto wonders: I should take them off: but then my socks would be a ruin. I should go barefooted through the city like a prophet. But then I'd hurt myself: Better off with dirty shoes.

He determines this while facing City Hall.

He is standing in the rubble of the excavation in the forecourt of La Seo. Because of all this digging-up his telephone has failed to function for eleven years so he feels not only angry at the mess the excavation makes of his black shoes he also feels he's owed an explanation. For the telephone. So he goes nearer to the edge of the big hole, leans over and peers into it. This being Spain there's no fence erected to protect the passersby from falling in, only an *aviso: ten cuidado!* "Careful," someone whispers next to him. But Modesto leans down even more. There's something going on down there: a noise like from a *palomar,* he thinks, the noise a hundred doves will make while sleeping, that low bubbling in their throats, the noise that comes from dovecotes as night falls.

"Friday prayers," he hears somebody whisper near him.

"*Qué?*" Modesto asks.

He looks around.

A voice from nowhere tells him, "From the mosque. The prayers at sundown. Friday is the Holy Day."

"What are you talking? Holy nothing; *look!*" Modesto points: "There's nothing there—!"

Suddenly the nightly conflagration in the sky begins again—huge bursts of color—and such thunder *eeiyy!*—and from the bottom of the excavation hundreds—thousands— wings—transparent—panic at the fireworks and beat around Modesto's face until they merge into a single swarm and beat away, unseen, toward heaven.

His father had once told him that he'd never feel the weight of his own body until he'd held a corpse, but Modesto thought that was just another of his father's lies because he'd felt his full and total weight the first time he had tried to fly.

The truth is: he had never made it off the ground. He had climbed some towers, but. He had climbed into the domes of the basilica of El Pilar each Saturday when he was still a boy but then they stopped him doing that because the stairs were falling down. For years now no one went there but the birds. Modesto knows their shit and molt are all that's holding the basilica together. Perhaps the fireworks will finally knock it down. Modesto hopes: then people will sit up and notice. He's feeling sickatheart because he's failed. He's failed to end the fireworks. The proof is this: the fireworks go on all night.

In the city packed with pilgrims he has lost his way in efforts to avoid them and it's nearing midnight when he finally climbs the crumbling stairs at No. 7 Plaza de Justicia to the third floor corner rooms. Outside his door he stops to wonder why there's no light on in the corridor. His stomach rumbles. *Eeiyy* he's so lightheaded he can't tell if he is seeing spots or not, it's pitchblack but for one high window through which the rhythmic crimson glare of fireworks is seen. The electric bulb is shattered in its socket so Modesto fumbles with the lock, no lock at all, a piece of string through catches where there used to be a bolt, which Modesto ties into a knot on leaving. Now Modesto's fingers fail him and he shuts his eyes to concentrate. He sees three round and perfect dots go floating by. There is a loud noise in the sky, the fireworks, and then he sees three dashes. He thinks his eyes are open now but still he sees three dots again. His fingers tear the string apart.

Inside his rooms it's very still, the walls are bathed in periodic light of the explosions in the sky. The doors that lead onto the balcony are standing open even though he thinks he closed them, as he always does, on leaving. Every pane of glass in them is broken. From the sky there comes another huge explosion and Modesto sees three things at once: First that light is a transparent substance; second that the sky is falling; third:

The bodies of his birds are motionless, together, at the bottom of their cage.

What kind of soul has he, Modesto starts to wonder, then he finds they weigh so little in their death he sinks onto a chair and puts their bodies on his knees. He sits there a long time and stares up at the sky above the city. The fireworks continue and the telephone begins to signal. After a while Modesto turns a bag of millet over, out onto the balcony. He tosses seeds into the street and some up toward the sky. His tears feel like the seeds themselves, hard against his eyes.

Soon birds arrive. They drop onto the balcony and tap their beaks against the seeds. Some gather on Modesto's lap. Some perch along his shoulders. The telephone keeps signaling. The sky explodes in a chaotic rhythm. Tap. Tap tap. The birds are feeding: *tap*. Modesto doesn't hear the voice behind him ask, "A last time please? The signals you are sending? In the sky? Each night? What are they asking for?"

Modesto doesn't feel the weight descend on him at all.

All he hears is tapping, tapping as they feed around him, *tap*.

It's like the signal that a ship sends when it's sinking, Modesto thinks: the birds and all this tapping: SOS.

He doesn't know what stands behind him.

Modesto wouldn't recognize an angel anyway.

Someday the world will end this way, he's thinking at the instant that the angel reaches him: Then *eso es*, that's that.

What kind of soul has he who cannot save the thing he loves?

LONDON
JANUARY 1990

BALLOONS 'N' TUNES

I'LL TELL YOU WHAT IT DOES, alright, it messes with your brain. It gets in there and cuts it up. That's the truth of what it does. It cuts you up. People ain't born crazy, see. Even people like them morons what you call them catatonics, they's born diminished, sure, but not born crazy. Crazy, see? Like sick and psychopathic. Like what happened to Joe Dean, right here adjacent to our own backyard. You think Joe Dean was born that way? No sirree Joe Dean was not born with his brain cut up. People ain't born crazy. That's what I believe. Other people and the facts of life combine to make them go that way but they ain't born that way, that's what you would say if you was here in person, that's what you would say. Balloons 'n' Tunes. Okay. Let's tune in to the radio. Let's tune in to K-nine-five. K-ninety-five. Your Tidewater Country. Your Con-tin-u-ous Country Station. Let's turn on the radio. Let's turn it on. Let's call our favorite Country in. Balloons 'n' Tunes. Let's call it in. Let's drive down to the A&N 'n' get the *Richmond Times Dispatch*. Let's drive on down. Let's drive down in the truck to A&N and get the *National Enquirer*. Let's go. Well, howdee, howdee, howdee. I'll take these two here papers. One for me and one for . . . howdee, howdee, I'll just take these two here papers. ELVIS' FIRST GRANDCHILD! Say! That's a history-makin' story, ain't it? That's a story 'n' a half! BLOCKBUSTER PHOTOS PLUS DRAMATIC STORY! What'd I tell ya? Some dramatic story, don't ya say? PLUS BABY DANIELLE'S EXCLUSIVE HOROSCOPE! Well, every baby's got to have one, don't ya say? True story, pet. True story just you bet. ACCIDENTAL DISCOVERY MAY END OBESITY! What's this? "A bore is somebody who talks when you want him to listen." Modern wisdom. ARAB MAN AND ISRAELI WIFE DEFY DEATH THREATS TO STAY TOGETHER IN BRU-TAL MIDEAST! True story, pet. Hey, did I tell ya I telephoned those Mertzes? Yep. I telephoned 'em. In Saluda, you re-member. I called them up. Caspar 'n' his stunning missus Spanky. People with such dang fool names. I called them up last week. Well, why not? They was family, weren't they? 'N' they hadn't called or nothin'. Purely nothin', so I called them up. I mean, family, Marl, you expect to hear from family even if the person is named Caspar. Spanky, you can just forget. But Caspar, I could buy a drink for someone with the name of Caspar but I wouldn't trust a dog named Spanky to behave with any delicacy, let alone a growed up woman by that name. Anyway they didn't even send a card or call or make a contribution even though Saluda takes the local paper and they must'a seen your name but, nevertheless, I called 'em willin' to extend the benefit 'a doubt that maybe they was out a town or doin' some strange thing that Caspars or that Spankys do that keep 'em occupied away from readin' papers 'n' I had to phone 'em umpteen different times 'til then one night I don't remember the exact time Caspar picks up the ol' phone real incensed like it had rung and interrupted him at prayin' 'n' I guess the gist of it was that I'd rung a little late 'n' he was sound asleep in bed owin' to being real ex-

hausted from whatever dang thing Caspars do. Real estate, I
think. The man sells real estate. "Caspar Mertz dash Real-a-
tor." I remember now he stuck his biz-ness card into my face
one time at an outdoor barbecue like it was gold or somethin'
useful. Solid gold. So there I was wakin' Caspar up to give
him my bad news and what he says next, he says, "I'm sorry,
Carl, that I ain't written you nor nothin' but the truth is
Spanky and me ourselves have been in a dee-cline these few
months." In a dee-cline. Hear me, Marl? It's like I never
thought of Caspar Mertz as bein' kin of your'n until he said
that dee-cline. Before he spoke that word I thought for sure
you was the only person on the planet that says dee-cline in
that way but there he was a distant kin of your'n talkin' in
that way I'd come to think was purely yours. Like I used to
say, "Where's that pie left over from last night?" 'n' you'd
say, "It's in the dee-frost, Carl." Then you'd say, "I'd like to
die from all this heat. I'd like to pay a billion dollar ransom
just to climb inside that dee-frost for a little while myself."
You used to always suffer in the heat, you used to always say,
"Big women always do." Why'd we stay our lives down
here in this heat, I'd like t' know, when we could'a lived
somewhere much cooler, Marl? Pennsylvania. I'd liked t'
lived in Pennsylvania. I could'a taken well to Philly. It's a
baseball town. But no you said, "I ain't livin' in a place
what's got its fame made from a brand 'a cream cheese." And
another thing: Why didn't we never take out health insurance? I'll tell 'ya why. You didn't like the salesman's shoes.
Why didn't we never turn on the air conditioner in the bedroom once for fifteen years? You were afraid you'd catch
some Legionnaire's. You and Your Reasons, Marl. Notice
who of us was always givin' in on issues such as these, Marlene. Just notice if you would, please, Marl. I could go in
there right now 'n' turn that a.c. down to sub-antarctic
weather just to please myself but I won't do that. Notice?
Have you asked yourself, "Why doesn't Carl go in and turn

that a.c. down to sub-antarctic weather?" Just think about it, Marl. Just give it a quick think. All your life you suffered from the heat. Seems like sometimes in the summer you was housin' 'lectric fans like they was orphans 'n' the two of us was ministers of charity. One time we must'a owned at least three dozen 'lectric fans. I couldn't read the paper 'less I laid it flat across the table what with all the hot air breezin' through the house. Still every night you had to sleep aneath a blanket. "Don't like sleepin' without cover," you would say. "Like to feel some weight atop me equal to a portion 'a myself." "Why don'sha wear a fur coat while you're at it?" I would say. " 'Cause someone I could mention never bought me one," you'd say. "Well, trade your 'lectric fans in, then, why don'sha? You got a fortune sittin' here in 'lectric fans. Orville Wright and Wilbur could'a blowed off to the moon with what you've got a-circulating in 'n' out'a here." "Now don't go findin' fault with me, Carl T., just because I like the look 'a breeze," you'd say. "The 'look 'a breeze'?" I'd say. "The 'look 'a breeze'?" What does breeze look like, Marlene? Go ahead 'n' tell me. What does breeze look like? Go on. I'm waitin'. Is there breeze in here? How can you tell or not if breeze is in the house if you can't see it? Huh? Go on. You tell me. You talk now. I been talkin' a blue streak. What does breeze look like? Marlene? I'm askin' for an answer, Marl. You gonna answer? I sit here 'n' I do all the talkin' 'n' what do you remember, I would like to know, not one damn thing. What news do you deliver? I sit here 'n' read you out the headlines from the papers 'n' all you do is nothin', big girl. I even read you out your daily horryscope 'n' I don't even know where you is at. Where are you, Marl? Is you in the atmosphere? Is you hangin' on some breeze? Is you sailin' in the universe? Is you—

"Who you talkin' to in there, Carl T.? I know you're in there, I can hear you talkin'."

Jest sit still. It's jest that pokey nose Dolores.

"Carl? Carl, I brought you over a hot meal."

She-*it*. My lips is glued together. My ass is glued down on this chair. Don't stand up, Carl T. Jest don't you answer, boy. Don't move. Too late. Dolores clatters in. Dolores is delivered like a sack 'a somethin' tossed onto a dock aside a ship. She sort of falls, like she was slung, into the kitchen. "Somethin' stinks like sour milk in here," she says.

"Excuse me while I fetch my legal rights," Carl says. He starts leafin' through the Yellow Pages book that's open on his lap. "Or don't you understand the concept of the word 'Trespassin' '?"

" 'Hullo' to you, too, Carl. Gawd, it's like an oven in here. It's all these in-can-descent bulbs. You should switch to low-heat bulbs. Why are all these lights on, anyway? You got every light on in the house." She puts a plate of somethin' wrapped up in a dishrag on the kitchen table and looks real tetchy at the nearly empty bottle of Tennessee mash sittin' there in front of him. "What's this?" Carl asks. He lifts the dishrag ladylike between his thumb and index finger and an aroma like an open can of dogfood hits his face. "This smells like doggie-do. What the heck is this here runny stuff?"

"I never seen you drinkin' mash before. Fact is, I never seen you drink a'tall."

"There's a lot 'a things you never seen me do which doesn't cancel out the fact I do 'em. You ever seen me make my armpit fart?" He slides his hand aneath his shirt which is open down the front because one morning he woke up and all the buttons had been tore clean off. He cups his palm into his armpit then he flaps his wing and makes his armpit fart. Dolores folds her arms across her chest and looks at Carl and sees he looks all wrong. He looks like somewhere that you know real well right after it's been wrecked by a bad storm. He moves the phone book from his lap and ties the dishrag 'round his neck, then he messes with the food she's brought.

"What's this?" he asks her, pointin' with the plastic spoon.

"That's mash potato, Carl, what'd you think it was?"

"Why's it gone all runny-like?"

"I must 'a added too much oil."

"There's oil inside these mash?"

"A bit too much. I guess."

"Oil, Dolores?"

"Liquid Crisco. It's supposed to be the lowest in them polywhatchumcalits."

"No one in their right mind puts oil in mash potato, Dolores. No one in the history of the world has ever put oil in mash potato, that's a fact, Dolores." He scoops up her drippy mash with the plastic spoon and glops it onto the plate and she just watches him. At any moment, she can feel, he might fling a spoonful of it somewhere, like at her, or like against the wall, or at the ceiling. She sort of flicks her eyes around the room for targets and that's when she sees what's hangin' in the window 'n' she looks away from it real quick. For the sake of normal conversation she says, "Well, what're you supposed to put in mash potato?"

"Milk," he says. "Pat 'a butter 'n' some pot likker. Never *oil,* Dolores. What is *this* disgustin' stuff?"

"Pork chops, Carl."

"How come they's gray?"

"*I* don't know how come they's gray. They wasn't always gray. They was pink-like when I bought 'em. Gray is just the color that they turned when they was cooked."

"You didn't, by any chance, boil 'em, did you?"

"No, actually, I stuck 'em in the micro-wave."

Carl's eyes take on a film of shine like they'd been lacquered.

"The micro-wave," he says.

"I got one free with my at-home job. They gave it to me. I got this job last week where I'm a random taster. I don't have to eat a lot or nothin', just take random tastes. I can do it any time 'a day. They say I'm the most micro-wave-friendly random taster in their em-ploy. I report directly to the senior manager of creative food services and no other random taster does that." Carl seems preoccupied so Dolores rattles on. "All the newest foods are aimed directly at the micro-wave—micro-wavable snack foods 'n' shelf-stable packaged foods. I read a bro-chure where they say that pretty soon micro-waves will even come in cars. The bro-chure said the micro-wave has had the most im-pact in this decade on the nation's eating habits. It says the kitchen is these days a warmin' center 'stead of bein' what it used to be, you know, some place to cook."

Carl slowly reaches for the bourbon bottle and starts playin' with its lid which he sees disturbs Dolores so even though his hand is shakin' he pours a goodly portion out into his dirty glass. " 'N' what's *this?*" he says, pointin' to a yellow circle with a red thing in the middle.

"Don't rile me, Carl, any fool can see that that's a ring a' pineapple."

" 'N' the red thing?"

"That's a mara-schino cherry 'n' you know it is. I thought the two together ought to add a small Ha-waiian touch."

"Well, you are a real creative genius, Dolores."

He sticks the handle of the plastic spoon into the chop as if it were a gravesite marker.

"You're bein' awful mean tonight," Dolores says like she is talkin' to a two-year-old. " 'N' all I done was come here with a hotdish."

"*Trespassed*," Carl reminds her.

"You could at least eat somethin' on that plate. Out 'a politeness."

Carl pops the maraschino cherry in the glass of bourbon, then he scarfs it down.

"I know you ain't never drunk in years," Dolores says.

"I know you ain't never drunk or else Marlene'ad told me."

"How do you know what I ain't never done? You weren't exactly Marlene's foremost trusted confidante, you know, Dolores."

"Well maybe not. Maybe that's entirely true. Maybe Marlene only ever talked to me to be polite. But she told me how come you had to stay in Massachusetts for a spell. She told me how you had to take The Pledge. 'N' Marlene never lied. You can say a lot 'a things about her but she never lied."

"*Marlene was not a dwarf.*"

"Gawd, Carl, I think you've fried your raisins."

"*Marlene is in the atmosphere.*"

"I think you've gone over the mountain. I think you're zoomin' straight downhill."

"Yep, I'm on a *dee*-cline, little lady. What you starin' at?" Dolores's eyes have flicked again to what is hangin' in the window and this time she's not alarmed to stare at it. "Ain't you never seen a lady's brazie hangin' from a window lock before?"

"To tell the truth, Carl, it's a little strange."

"Well, think about it. Just give it a quick think, Dolores."

"I don't think I want to, Carl, the whole thing is too weird." Still, she can't stop lookin' at it. The bra is hangin' from the window lock at about the height Marl's breasts had been. The back is hooked, the straps are looped over the hanger and the cups are all puffed out.

"I had it hangin' on the doorknob for a while," Carl says, " 'n' then I looked at it one day 'n' said, 'This isn't right. *Marlene was not a dwarf.*' That's when I moved it over to the window, see. Bit of native inspiration. I looked around for somethin' near the height 'a Marl 'n' there it was. The window. You should see it when the sun shines through. You ought 'a come around sometime when the sun is out 'n' see the shadow it can make across the floor."

Dolores looks up toward the ceiling where the moths are gathering around the kitchen light. Dead flies are silhouetted in its globe. She looks like she is strugglin' to find courage from the insect congregation, then she pulls a breath of hot close air 'n' says, "I think you need to seek some help, Carl T. I dearly do. I think you need to seek a preacher. Or better still, I got some names of doctors in a drawer back home."

"Stick 'em in your micro-wave, Dolores."

"I'm not speakin' lightly, Carl." She waits to draw some more hot air. "I been through this kind'a strife before. I been through a mental breakdown with Joe Dean remember. 'Course with you I can't be sure what's talkin' here is mental strife or one man's whiskey."

"Thank you very much for callin' 'round, Dolores."

Carl starts flippin' through the pages of the Yellow Pages book.

"Have you heard a single word I've spoken, Carl?"

"Yes, ma'am. I'm much beholden' t' you. You've reminded me I need t' go and buy myself more whiskey."

"You're a threat to other motorists the way you are right now."

"You drive out 'n' buy it for me, then."

"You know that I don't drive."

"Alrightee, I'll drive out 'n' buy it then."

"Or maybe I'll do somethin' first. You think Marl never took me into con-fi-dence. Well let me tell you this. If that's the case how do I know to do what Marl would do if she was here? How do I know she used to put your locomotion to a standstill every time you got like this? How do I know that all I have to do to disappoint your travel plans is go out to the truck 'n'—"

Carl begins to flap his wing and make his armpit fart in quick succession like the sound of someone clapping.

Dolores stops and stares at him.

When he's done with makin' fun of her he says, "She

learned me long ago I oughtn't start to drink unless I had it in control."

He lifts one cheek from off the chair and draws a knobby-lookin' thing from his rear pocket. "The distrib'orator cap," he says.

"I could still go out 'n' let the air out all the tires."

"I could blow them up no problem."

"I could call a social welfare worker."

" 'N' say what? 'A man is drinkin' in his domicile'? 'A man is feelin' sorry for his self in his own kitchen'?"

"It's been this way for somethin' like six months."

"I know how long it's been."

"You need to pull yourself together."

"I know what I need."

"You have to think what she would feel if she could see you in a state like this."

Carl looks up at her.

"I know how she'd feel," he says. "If Marl was here she would feel merciful 'n' sorry. Somethin' *you* don't feel, Dolores."

"Don't try 'n' make me feel ashamed," Dolores says real slowly. "You know as well as I do I'm as lonely in my way for Marl as you are, Marl was like a momma to me."

"She didn't see too much of your devotion near the end there, did she, now, Dolores?"

Dolores flushes and she feels like she could go at him. "That's just plain unkind 'a you. You know as well as I do I had troubles with Joe Dean back then."

"Jest so long as you can live with it," Carl states.

"That's a spiteful poison thing t' say," she says. "It seems t' me you ain't exactly rollin' in congratulants yourself."

"Is that a fac'? Just what do you imagine that I've done the world could blame me for? Sittin' with her all those days 'n' keepin' watch while she departed in such pain?"

Dolores looks down at the floor where there's two roaches runnin' at his shoes.

"Watchin' her go down t' nearly nothin'—'n' I mean *nothin'* here, Dolores—'til I hardly knew if Marl was in that heap 'a bones a'tall or if she'd clear e-vaporated?" he demands.

"I think I'd ought'a push on back t' where I came from," she says softly.

" 'N' take your plate 'a runny mash potato with you."

She finds it near impossible to look at him. She lifts the plate up with one hand, her back turned toward him. "What about my dishrag?" she asks 'n' stops 'n' turns around 'n' looks at him 'n' sees that tears are streamin' from his eyes. Next thing she knows she's stormin' 'cross the backyard toward her house 'n' throwin' the whole plate out into the darkness. Somewhere, not too far away because she's muscularly undeveloped, she hears it come down in the dry grass that he hasn't mowed for half a year. She stops and stands and wonders how she's going to find it, then she hears him talkin' so she turns around. *Who's he talkin' to?* she wonders so she goes to see. The back door is still open like she left it 'n' the light is shinin' through. She squats down on the backstoop in the dark and listens.

"Alma-Dial-A-Miracle," he's sayin', "see? I got the ad right here. Where's it at? Right here. Page forty-six. The *National Enquirer*. It's in the Classifieds. ALMA-DIAL-A-MIRACLE. RESULTS ALL PROBLEMS. RETURNS LOVED ONES. See? 'N' look, look, here—Alma's got two codes. Y' see? You see this here? Two numbers listed here for Alma with two codes like Alma's in two places all at once! Convincin', ain't it, 'less it's some danged place, you know, where there's a single residence astride two dialin' codes. 713 'n' 213. Let's look it up. Let's give ol' Alma th' ol' time 'a day. I was just about t' look it up before that pokey pokey what's herbones showed up, okay, okay, we got it here, this 213, we got it here inside this Yellow Pages book, okay, well, 213 appears to be Los Angeles 'n' 713 . . . seven-one-three . . . well, seven-*zero*-three as we both know is right here in Virginia, yes indeedee, got us here the Yellow Pages map. Divide the Country up by Codes. No States. Just Codes. Alrightee. Well. You'd think they might'ad laid it out numerically, but no. They cut it up. The map. It cuts you up. Well 712, that's seven-twelve, that's Council Bluffs in Iowa we've never been to I-o-wa, so we'll keep on lookin'. Seven 'n' its mate thirteen. Seven hunderd 'n' thirteen. Here it is, y' see it, Marl? It's Houston. Houston, Texas, Marl, well I'll be glabbed, I'm sayin' *Houston,* shit, well I'll be splatter'd. Houston. Alma-Dial is at one time receivin' calls in Houston, Texas, Marl, 'n' at the same time takin' calls at her place 'a biz-ness in Los Angeles, isn't that a miracle? Or what is that? Is that a miracle? Is this a mir-a-cle or what? Two places at one time. *Why* do I want t' get in touch with Alma-Dial-A-Miracle? *Why?* Marl? Well, I'll tell 'ya. First I like her Codes, I like her Codes, I like t' think 'a Alma in big cities. Secondly, I like her name. I chose her name against those others. In the *National Enquirer.* You know, these others here. Like this one, APRIL GENUINE AS-TROLOGER. April Genuine—what kind'a name is that? Or this one. REVEREND MOTHER RACHEL PSYCHIC. You begin to get my drift, here, SISTER CREST. SUSAN PSYCHIC. MR. KOMAR. Dingbat kind'a names I'm certain you agree. Can't trust important matters such as this to dingbats no sirree. You get my drift. Gott'a have the kind'a name that sounds ap-pro-pri-ate I'm sure you will agree. Always had a thing for names. My 'hick' thing you called it. One more symptom of my natural 'hick'-ness comin' as I do from 'hick'-town U.S.A. Well can I help it people where I came from all had names that told you who they was? Turner Round. I told you about Turner Round. God knows what name her momma gave her at her birth but she was ugly as a coondog all her life so people took to shoutin' 'Turn 'er 'round!' every time she came within their focus so it stuck, the name, just like True Story Pet. You remember ol' True Story, don'sha? Crazy as a she-goat in a shit-house she would tell you her life story front to back each time she caught you in the road and every time she told it she would end with tellin' you, 'True story, pet,' despite the fac' it came out diff'ernt every time she told it, diff'ernt times 'n' places, diff'ernt fac's 'n' such. 'N' Mashie was called Mashie once't his hand went down the thresher so sure, you know, you know, I have a sort'a del-i-cate re-la-tion-ship with names, historic'ly I mean, I mean, I have a hist'ry in them so this Alma, here, this Alma-Dial sounds like she will fill the bill 'n' anyway she's got the Codes, two Codes, she's got two Codes where all the others have but one. *Why* do I need to get in touch with Alma? Well, I'll tell you, Marl, I think we need her to get through to you. I purely do. Owin' to th' fac' that I can't figure where you are. Balloons 'n' Tunes. Can't figure it a'tall. The thing is this—I need t' talk with you, big girl. We need t' have a conversation. I need t' get this off my chest for once. About that end, there, Marl. About the end. See I've been thinkin' that I never should'a let you have your say, that maybe you were not yourself, you were clearly not yourself, that maybe you were not yourself with all that pain. You read me? So far? Marl? No in-sult to you, you held up held up like th' gift 'a God right through there 'til the end but since, you see, since then I have been thinkin' 'n' I think that I was wrong to let you have your final say of what was done. I think that I was truly wrong because I can't make sense of it no matter what. You never liked th' heat 'n' that's a fac'. You suffered it 'n' all the while that I was doin' it I knew it wasn't right. I went in there 'n' I don't know what it was that I expected. The gentleman he says to me, 'Can you come back, please, in two hours, Mister Tanner?' 'What for?' I says to him. 'Missus Tanner's ashes will be ready in two hours . . .' "

On the porch stoop, in the night, Dolores hugs her knees up to her chin because she's feelin' cold.

"Comes out lookin' like the stuff you get there at the

bottom of a vacuum cleaner," Carl is sayin'. "I put it in a freezer bag, the kind that is see-thru. They were pushin' fancy items at me, you know, silv'ry orn-a-ment-al things, those whatchacallum's, things that horses win at races, trophy-lookin' things like vases, fancy goods when we was never fancy people in our lives, you know, so I said, 'Keep 'em,' 'n' I took it in a freezer bag 'n' drove around while thinkin' what t' do. *Somewhere nice 'n' pretty,* you had said. So I drove down to the river, naturally, the Appomattox, knowin' you had always favored that par-tic-u-lar-ly ugly twisty skinny yellow river to the James—just drove out toward that group'a islands there around Fort Clifton 'n' the White Banks, lookin' for a spot, for somewhere nice 'n' pretty, thinkin' to myself *Her will be done.* After a while I drove 'round to that overview at Point of Rocks there in that turnoff over Sunken Island 'n' I sat there for a while. This is where I think we're in the wrong. I truly do. Balloons 'n' Tunes. See I didn't know that was the last time that we'd be together. Somewhere nice 'n' pretty. I didn't know that it had come t' purely nothin'. Purely nothin', Marl. I didn't know that was the last time we would ever be alone together. It was nice 'n' pretty like you asked. I got out from the truck 'n' walked a little ways out toward the bluff with that there freezer bag. Nothin' happened then it seemed the time t' do it had arrived. I think my mind was empty 'cause I didn't know. I didn't know what it would mean. So what does breeze look like, Marlene? How do you know a breeze is comin' at you if the plain fac' is it can't been seen? I flapped the, you know, bag, expectin' it would fly there toward the river, when a breeze come up, 'n' there you went, girl, all behind me and above me where the road turns past the scenic view, this van, delivery van, comes barrelin' along, 'Balloons 'n' Tunes.' This van, a little white one, Japanese. It's like I can see the whole thing, right here, just in front 'a me, this guy turns on his windshield wipers. Not that there was much. There wasn't much. He must'a seen it, though. He turns his windshield wipers on. On the side it says, 'Balloons 'n' Tunes.' He's doin' maybe forty, fifty miles an hour 'n' he's there 'n' gone 'n' turns his windshield wipers on 'n' that was that. 'N' that was that. The thing was there 'n' gone. You see. What kind'a thing is that? Marlene? What kind'a name is that? Balloons 'n' Tunes. What's that? Names 'a things there in the air. Names 'a things that go by in the air . . ."

Outside Dolores looks up at the sky and thinks, not for the first time, *shit. The world is just a gross and slimy place.*

Then, before she goes back in she even says it, right out loud.

WELSH BORDERS
JULY 1989

EVOLUTION

WELL WHAT SHE WAS DOING in the kitchen at that hour of the night was on account of Goodie Benz telling her this story Goodie claimed Ray Bradbury had written about the final ending of the world. Vy has never even read the story and knowing how Goodie says she lives with gnomes behind her wall there's a good chance Goodie hasn't read it either. What I mean is maybe Goodie made it up. This is not your average possibility beyond your average doubt because Goodie has that witch's way with words, that is to say she makes them all sound true, so anyway about this story that maybe Ray Bradbury once wrote: there's this radio announcement that the world is coming to an end. In the story the way Goodie told it (and the way that Vy remembers it) some jackass has gone ahead and ordered up 300 megatons to detonate over Omaha Nebraska which means The End. In 20 minutes. A love story. So anyway the hero and the heroine in the story are this old married couple and they decide they'll go lie down on the bed and wait for The End to come and die in each other's arms. Maybe Goodie didn't say they were an *old* couple, but Vy imagines them that way. So they go into the bedroom and the clock is ticking and they hold onto one another tight. Vy imagines an apartment somewhere out in Brooklyn on the way to Coney Island under the El-evated but she may have gotten this mixed up in her mind with *Sophie's Choice* or some Woody Allen movie. Anyway in Vy's mind there's this old couple out in Brooklyn and the sun is streaming through the windows and maybe there's a gentle breeze lofting a lace curtain on the street side and life as we have known it since day-1 is on the launching pad and the countdown's started and the count is 2. Suddenly the old gal stirs. "Where are you going?" the old guy who's her husband in this story asks. "I'll be back in just a minute," she assures him, then gets up like she's a sleepwalker. About this time the count is down to 1. The old gal says, "I have to go and check. I think I hear the faucet dripping."

Now this story is that kind of thing like tunes or radio commercials that once they gain a foothold on the *cuesta* of your conscious thought you can forget about your ever being free again which explains how we get Vy downstairs at that hour of the night twisting sink knobs in the kitchen just as Cicely her daughter tumbles in. "Uh oh," says Cis. "You caught me."

"Wuz you on the fly?" Vy asks.

Vy, a person of impeccable finesse in her pill-puckered chenille robe, does not usually start questions off with *wuz*, but the Island Theatre Workshop (hereafter called the "ITW") was putting on the 3-Act *Optimizm Hertz* about the first black Jewish woman President of the United States from Florida and Vy has the lead role of Miz Hertz and to get into a southern female, though not Jewish, frame of mind she'd been reading all day from the collected stories of Eudora Welty whom she got a kick out of by referring to as *Y'all*-dora Welty; ergo, *wuz*. But "Uh oh," she now notes, turning a bald eye on Cis. Cis doesn't look herself. In fact, Cis looks *tight*. Vy's heart sinks like a dull stone through a pawnshop window in a felony: "You *wuz* on the fly; yes, you wuz," she submits. Her sad heart thwacks its cage like a lovesick bird. "How was the party—fine?" she asks a bit too loudly, just a bit. She knows you never tip your hand to children; never, never let-them-in-the-know. *Don't let the kid see your internal pit-a-pat* is Vy's maternal motto. Stay calm and stay cool, the best mothers always do, so what if Cis is just 14—? There's a couple options open to you Vy, Vy thinks, and one of them involves a weapon you refuse to own on the grounds that it kills people and the other one involves the kind of travel luggage that you haven't got. Her rage and disappointment clamor in her bloodstream like steam perking in the whatsis of an overheated car. "Cis. You're. Pissed," she whistles.

"I am not," Cicely maintains. "Hold it hold it hold it right there just a minute," she insists. She leans against the chair back, misses, topples chair and six tangelos to the floor and says, "Look. See? Listen. I know exactly what I'm saying." She points to her mouth, misses, stares quizzically at her fingertip and says, "The room is going 'round."

Vy by this time forgets about Eudora Welty and her optimizm. One of the tangelos has rolled over for a visit at her feet and she is thanking her Creator for small things such as not having to have to play this scene with pineapples as they would have knocked her senseless and left weird fruit scratches around her ankles like some rodent had died attempting to shimmy itself up her foreleg.

"It was cool, Vy," says Cicely. "We were playing quarters? The game where you bounce to get in?" (Cicely as we know is 14 and makes sentences like this: Vy, in school today? Mr. Giannitti cracked us up? He said how many kids does it take to shingle a roof. 2? Sliced very thin?) "And since this was my first party everybody ranked on me. I got it in once? I passed it to Katy? God." She sits. She sits on a tangelo which has rolled to rest in the crater of the kitchen chair but she doesn't notice. "Vy what's abong?"

Vy squints. She should have named this child "Anita" like she wanted. A daughter named "Anita" would put away six margaritas, dance her tootsies off on rooftops and bring grief and desolation to the *federalistas,* not to Vy. "How much beer do you think you had exactly Cicely?" Vy asks.

"I don't know, six glasses I guess but they were little glasses? Plus toward the end they were mostly full of other people's spit. Abong?"

"*Wha*—?"

"Chinese thing it looks like? Big vase with hoses everybody blowing on them?"

"O. A Bhang."

"There was one of them."

"O. Great."

"I don't know, it was great? I'm really learning stuff, you know?"

"O great."

"Like people who drink beer and wine? They get rosy and their eyes get shiny and they sparkle?"

Despite herself, Vy pines.

"But the people? Some of them? Who took the other stuff? Boy, I don't know what they were taking but Sue? Her face got white."

"Her face got white?"

"Got white and her eyes they got like *this?* Both of them. Like little slits and she didn't seem too happy with her life? O well I have to call Dawn. She said there's something real important she must tell me."

Cicely stands up and walks into the counter. "Where's the phone."

"Behind you."

First there is (A Pause.)

Then there is (Confusion.)

"On the wall," Vy says.

"O!" Cicely realizes.

This statement is perhaps the funniest that Cis has heard since Vy's talk about the foam and condoms. The fact that she has lost the phone?

"Ha! Ha! Ha!" Cis laughs.

"Listen Cis before you make the call I need to know one thing. Are you going to puke?"

Cis checks her forehead with the flat part of her hand. "Don't think so, no. Vy. Will you dial?"

"I'm serious Cicely. Listen. Are you listening? There's a chance you're going to feel like puking. I mean *really* puking. Like tossing all your walnuts."

"Vy will you hold this while I have to go and pee."

"Did you dial?"

"I don't remember."

"What's the number?"

Cis calls from the bathroom "6-9-3 no wait a minute 6-9-3-4-7-4-7-4-7—how many numbers is that—8-2. But if her mother answers, Vy hang up? That's what I do."

So Vy dials. The phone rings while she's looking at her kitchen. No cockroaches, *that's* a godsend.

"Hello, Dawn? This is Vy, Cicely's mother? Fine, how are you? What? O sure, go ahead . . ."

(A Rather Long Pause.)

"What's she saying—?"

"She put me on Hold so now I'm Holding."

"Now you're what—?"

"I'M HOLDING FOR GODSAKE HAS EVERY 14-YEAR-OLD ON THE PLANET EARTH BEEN CALLED BY ITS HIGHER POWER TO THE TOILET?"

"Ha! Ha! Ha!"

"Yes, I'm still here dear excuse me CICELY SHE'S BACK I'm sorry Dawn Cis will be with us in a moment ARE YOU COMING CIS?"

"I forgot what I'm doing."

"WELL HURRY UP."

"I forgot."

"CICELY DID YOU TAKE YOUR PANTS DOWN?"

(Another Long Pause Owing to On-Site Inspection.)

"Ha! Ha! Ha!"

"Dawn dear I'm going to go upstairs to bed now if you don't mind but when Cis comes to the phone will you give her a message from me dear? Thank you that's real kind. Will you tell Cis if she pukes in the middle of the night that's her tough luck? That's right. You heard. Helping people puke and watching people get injections are two things I can't stand. I never could so it must be in my genes. That and watching people eating greasy foodstuffs with their hands. CICELY ARE YOU MOVING SOON OR DO YOU WANT DAWN TO CALL YOU BACK?"

O God, Vy thinks as she lets the phone hang from its cord, Please don't let me come down in the morning to find the phone still hanging here and Cis sprawled in the toilet like a pooped puppet and all passed out and then me having only-You to haul her up these million stairs she weighs about 100 lbs.

Before Vy goes upstairs she gives a twist to each one of those drippy faucets and feels much better for it. Optimizm once more occupies her mind. Who knows? If I do real good in this part, she thinks, I might even get a chance to play the lead in next season's verse-play up-date of *Gone with the Wind*—*O Rhett! I know you've gone to Delhi far away* Vy rehearses her Atlanta accent as she climbs the stairs, *But even when it's Tuesday there and Monday here // "Tomorrow" is "another" day* (Applause.)

As if it's even likely that she'd wake
up in the morning

dead
dumb
blind
comatose
with a low I.Q.

Vy scribbles notes the night before. This morning's reads:

"Before blaming

maggots
sharks
gannets
snakes
piranha
fish

for being created

maggots
sharks
gannets
snakes
piranha
fish

ask
yourself

WHAT'S SO GREAT ABOUT YOU—?"

And then on top of that she remembers dreaming about mutagens in frozen foods again.

Mutagens you will remember are those little chemical whatsos that cause changes in genetic throne rooms of our cells by mechanisms still unknown. This was in the *New York Times* last week dateline MADISON WISCONSIN so you know it's not elitist Northeast crap. It, the article, imparted unto Vy unwanted information about frying doughnuts and onion rings and tacos and french fries and fish sticks and frozen shrimp and chicken nuggets in beef fat and commercial cotton oil. The reason this was on Vy's mind while dreaming (she wouldn't on her *life* fry food in cotton oil!) the reason that the headline MADISON, WIS., Feb. 5 "MUTAGENS IN FRIED FOOD" stopped her in her daily scan of headline news is that Cicely has always loved fried food especially fried shrimp and fried potatoes. While most kids were still gumming Gerber peas Cis was chowing down french fries and shrimp. Now some pervert in Madison Wisconsin who has nothing better to do with his life than make trouble for mothers and fast-food franchise owners in the good ol' U.S.A. comes to the conclusion that in studying fries and onion rings no significant mutagen formation is found even after reusing the same oil 45 times (Even Vy knows a person is a psycho to use the same oil 45 times) but *but*! an increase in the level of mutagenic activity in the preparation of breaded fish and shrimp is evident when the oil is reused in the frying more than six times. Six times! Vy thinks. Who could be expected to remember if she's used the cooking oil that often? What if Cis is already mutagen-fucked-for-life? What if she Vy has spawned mutation in her own little powdered *fasnacht* of a girl—?

So down the hall Vy goes this morning and there's Cis in Cis's room. Cis who looks like Cis with not a sign of mutagenic activity. Still, looking like herself and free of mut. activity is one thing; good's another. Cis does not look good.

"Sick headache," Cis says through a pair of too-pale lips. "Tummy upset."

Here where another mother might rush in and say I told you so or Serves you right or *Ex oceano natabis* Vy steers the conversation toward herself: "ITW is coming over for a lox brunch and rehearsal," she says, "but we'll try to keep it quiet. H-o-n-e-y," she drawls, trying not to rock the raft that Cis is barely clinging to, "have I ever got this one godawful line in Scene 2 that kept me up all night. I have to say 'Galapagos' in a Southern accent and I can't. I have to say 'Galapagos is just another promontory in the sea of life' like I was from Atlanta or, well, no, *Daytona*, actually. I have to say it like 'GaLAPgiz' and my mouth just collapses like a barn around it, GLAPgiz . . . hold on a sec. WE'RE UP HERE!" Vy shouts.

Bells for Adano and Saint Mary's both resound ad nauseum around poor Cis's temples. Her stale mattress laps around her while the girl groans on her moorings. Then suddenly there's another person one more uninvited in her bedroom taking up its air.

"Hello darlings," this new person says. (These *theatre*

people! Vy can't keep herself from thinking.) "Listen love I got the *Sunday Times* and four bottles of fizzywine because I crave mimosas on a Sunday morning and I put it on your charge—O! Heavens above, just look! It's green! My god Vy what's the matter with It—?"

"It's hungover."

"Hahahaha good one Vy."

"No really. It's hungover."

"True. I'm going to puke."

"From what? Watching 'Mary Tyler Moore'?"

"Beer."

"Bite your tongue madwoman."

"Six or possibly six dozens of them," Vy explains. "It was dark. We can't be sure. Plus maybe other people's spit might figure in it."

From the rumpled depths of Cis's bed there emanates a pungent rumbling.

"That's it! It's coming," Cis moans, "stand back! It's starting in my tubes—!"

"Good grief." (Exit Theatre Person.)

"Your *tubes* Cis?"

"Sorry Vy. Some people had on too much English Leather."

"Well sit up anyway it's only in a fire that you're safer near the floor. Move over. That's better. I'll read the paper to you. O my god! What's this on the cover of the *Sunday Times Magazine*? Dinosaurs? It must be something riveting and must-know if it's on the cover."

"Really Vy I don't have the stomach for them."

"Come on Cis—"

"No Vy. I really don't. They look disgusting."

"Then I'll read you some descriptions from the camp advertisements you know how much you love the thought of camp . . . O Cis this stuff on dinosaurs is real hot stuff. Look at this!"

"What is it—? O!"

"Real hot stuff huh?"

"Yuk."

"It says here this one had a set of tiny 'articulated hands.' "

"They're gross . . ." (She peeks.) "What's *that* Vy?"

"An artist's rendering of what the experts say dinosaurs would have evolved to if they hadn't been wiped out."

"Doubleyuk."

"Well Cis they say that beauty's in the—"

"Slimy green skin."

"—eye of—"

"Pointy little lizard face."

"They *are* a bit unsavory."

"I'm going to puke Vy."

"I'll spread the Business Section out for that—what's *this*?"

"Can't see it, hold it up. O. Some stupid thing I had to write for English."

" 'A-minus'? What kind of grade is that? 'Good writing but I can't help wondering how Chekhov would have treated it'—? What kind of crack is that? Is this why I pay my taxes? Who cares how Chekhov would have treated it? Fact is he didn't. What's it about?"

"The final ending of the world."

"O Cicely you didn't steal the one about the drippy water faucet did you?"

"I didn't steal a thing. It's about these invaders from another galaxy who zap the world? Except they miss three people two men and a woman."

"I think I saw this one."

"Vy I'm telling you I made this up—"

"Is one of them Harry Belafonte?"

"Vy no listen one of them's a Chinese woman doctor, one of them's a pygmy from the Onge tribe and the last one's a transvestite. Eskimo."

"And your teacher wondered how *Chekhov* would have treated it? How do they meet?"

"Who."

"The Eskimo and Chinese woman doctor and—"

"O. They don't?"

"That's sad."

"Well that's the point Vy."

"The one with Harry Belafonte was a sad one too. I guess there's not a lot of comedy around after The End eh, Cis?"

Someone downstairs calls *Vy if I were you where would I find the snipped chives for the omelettes?* and Vy starts to leave but Cis says, "Who's Harry Belafonte Vy?" so Vy stops by the door and looks across at Cis who's looking better.

"Kind of a pop star," Vy explains.

"Nice name."

"O sure we went in for the names back then. Anita. Stella. Names like that."

"Yeah. Everyone was really into that Italian stuff back then weren't they Vy."

Vy's mouth falls open but no words pop out.

Cis says, "Like Madonna when you think of it is following tradition? With her name and stuff? A bunch of us had this real good conversation on it last night. At the party? We thought it would be really cool next year to take Italian Renaissance and you know catch up on the fifties?"

Sharply Vy's heart pinches. The sun breaks through the clouds on Cis's window lighting up her hair and in a twinkling Cicely her daughter a chrysalis dusts her wings as if she's stepped ashore amid the blue-gold razzles of a Botticelli painting that she's never seen. O lordy Vy exhales. Her heart begins to kick like a mountain kid across the lumpen moraine of her cleavage as she thinks No use in me pretending that the work I have to do is going to keep until another day because there'll never be another one and that's the truth. She means like this one. When it's gone. So she says, "Cis?

131

"Remember when we had that Real Talk honey?"

Cis says, "The one about food additives or the one about the Foam—?"

"Both. Now listen. There's something I forgot to tell you—"

"Vy can you put this on Hold I'm going to listen to a tape."

What happens next is (Stillness.)

Followed by (A Real Loud Noise.)

And that as Vy would like to say was how her daughter came to understand how much it takes to make an ordinary Mother change into a Lesson that you won't Forget.

MARTHA'S VINEYARD
AUTUMN 1981

REX

NOTHING WONDERFUL MAKES a phone call in the middle of the night, the northern lights don't ring you up to let you know they're coming. Lovers call, the former kind; the cops. People who speak words that don't go well together call you to make sounds that spell bad news. After midnight something happens to the air inside a telephone, it thins like winter light and things sound loud, they sound alarming, they make a sound designed to waken sleeping dogs.

The call that came was from her sister.

It was 12 midnight Atlantic Coast, 9 P.M. in San Francisco. Patricia had been woken in the middle of the night while, on the other side, Myra was just home from work, standing in her kitchen. Their other sister, Ellen, had rung Myra from New York, then Myra had rung Pat in Woods Hole, Massachusetts, from San Francisco. Lines were crackling all around and the news created its own circuit. The news was this: somewhere in the last eight hours their mother, traveling from coast to coast by air with two bags and one Pekingese, had gotten lost. She was seventy-six years old. She had white hair. No one in his right mind would ever kidnap Nina, Myra said. Myra was the one who'd put their mother on the plane in San Francisco. Don't talk that way, Patricia told her. There's been a mix-up. *She could be dead* they both were thinking.

The gist of it was this: a storm had massed over the Rockies, dumped a partial payload on the Plains and was heading towards the East Coast faster than a speeding bullet and somewhere either in the air or on the ground between San Francisco International Airport and La Guardia in New York there was a white-haired, seventy-six-year-old, five-feet-two-and-a-half-inches-tall woman answering to the name of "Mother" in their circumstances, "Nina" in most others; one royal blue two-suiter suitcase with a winter coat jammed in it and another royal blue suitcase not as big, not the same brand, not exactly matching the two-suiter's shade of blue, which was stuffed to bursting with wool socks, wool underwear, a flannel nightgown and presents for the grand-children; and, in a cardboard Porta-Kennel behind whose wire mesh his black eyes wept while his worm-colored tongue searched in vain for syllables . . . beloved Winston, Pekingese.

To say that Winston was an ugly dog did Winston kind. To say that he embodied all the meanest elements inherent in his breed and then to say his breed was Pekingese and Nina spoiled him rotten justified her daughters' certainty that no one in his right mind would try to waylay Nina for a chance to dognap Winston. The world was sick but not so sick it would abet harm to a white-haired woman for a chance to steal an ugly dog.

The sensible conclusion was they'd got lost.

Between two shores, among three daughters, amid no-body's airspace, over sacrosanct frontiers—California, Utah,

Colorado, Omaha, Des Moines, Chicago, Hershey Pennsylvania—they were lost. No terrorist would steal somebody over Utah, would he? Myra asked. Myra was the terrorist-freak, she'd canceled her vacation to Corfu because of Libyans: now *this*. Her own mother had gone out of sight in her own native land. Kidnapped, Myra breathed. *From thirty thousand feet?* Ellen insisted. *Someone jumped to safety from a Delta 747 over Nevada with Mother in his evil grasp and Winston in a Porta-Kennel?*

"The fact is," Ellen said, "you put Nina on the plane in San Francisco and when it landed at La Guardia she and Winston and her suitcases were nowhere to be found."

Oh no, Myra lamented, this isn't happening, this is impossible, do the airline people think it might be flying saucers?

Listen, Ellen said. For some reason—God knows what—when the airplane stopped in Denver Nina must have gotten off.

Does she *know* someone in Denver? Myra asked.

Don't you know? her sister asked. That's the *point*—*I* don't know who Mother knows. Don't *you* know who Mother knows? Who does Mother know?

She used to say she used to know what's-her-name, Ike's wife.

"Ike?"

The president.

"The president of what?"

Of the you-know. Country. Mamie.

"Mamie?"

With the bangs.

"The bangs?"

That one.

"This is the eighties—!"

I know that.

"Christ!"

It doesn't mean that they were meaningless.

"The *bangs*?"

The Eisenhowers.

"What do the *Eisenhowers* have to do with what we're dealing with, for christsake? What do *they* have to do with who Mother knows in Denver, Colorado? Who does Mother *know—that's* the issue. . . ."

Well, like I said, she used to say she knew Mamie Eisen—

"*Now*. Who does Nina know in Denver *now*?"

Denver, Myra answered. I wish this wasn't happening in Denver. Denver used to be among the ten best places in the world. I used to think of Denver as a nice place to fly into.

"No more," Ellen admitted. "Listen. I think we have to face the fact that Mother's sick," she said. "I'm not saying that it's time to panic, but I think we have to face the fact that evidence is mounting which sustains the proof that she's a victim of attack from the inside. . . ."

A *spy network*?

"Her *body*, dope."

"Oh cripes, but Nina's *fit*."

"Exactly what was Nina wearing?"

"*What*?"

"What did she have on, do you remember?"

"I don't like this, Ellen."

"Be a big girl, Myra, try to visualize it, you're the last person who saw her and I have to call a lot of hospitals and the police."

If I live to be a hundred years I won't forget you said that, Myra pledged her sister.

It was Ellen, then, who called the Delta Airline people out in Denver. She also called the Colorado State Police who were very nice and said they'd check the hospitals around the Denver area. The airline people weren't so nice. The storm, by then, had gotten pretty bad and it affected them. As far east as La Guardia airline people were forecasting air travel delays that gave them headaches. Everyone, it seemed, was nervous.

Myra called Pat in Massachusetts to give her the bad news and she and Pat agreed to stay beside their phones until, from somewhere, Nina would decide to call. Meanwhile none of them could keep from calling up the other two as hours passed and nothing happened and no word from Nina came. Around 4 A.M. that first night Ellen called Patricia to say she couldn't stand the wait anymore. She was going to La Guardia again in case Nina had arrived from Denver on another airline, she told Pat. "*That's stupid,*" Pat insisted.

They went over the description of what Myra said Nina had been wearing when she left: thick shoes.

What do you mean, "thick shoes"? Ellen had asked.

Nursies, Myra had said. "Opaque stockings."

Myra, I don't need a fashion essay.

A twill skirt.

What color?

Slate.

"*Slate,*" *for christsake?*

Okay, "gray."

On top?

Her Irish sweater.

Color?

Off-white, you know. "Creamy."

Hat?

What?

Was Nina wearing a hat?

No.

No hat?

No.

Sometimes she liked wearing hats.

Past tense?

What?

Never mind.

The hat?

She wasn't wearing one.

No?

No.

You're sure?

I'm sure.

You're positively sure?

I'm *sure*—she was wearing that little ponytail the way she does, with her elastic.

Winston?

What?

What was Winston wearing?

Oh. His Tartan. One of his bright plaids. His leather collar. I remember 'cause I said to Nina that the leather one looked nice and understated. For traveling, you know. Instead of that other artificial ruby one.

"*Holy Christ*," Pat said to Ellen when she heard this for the seventh time around 6 A.M. the morning of the second day. "Has anybody thought to check the *vets?*"

Pekingese is not a common breed in Denver and the first reports were many and confused. A Weimaraner by the name of Walther who'd been brought in by a woman answering Nina's description was believed by the State Police to be the missing Winston and the false discovery held the sisters in a state of anxiousness for several hours on the morning of the second day. "If someone really wants to," a Colorado state trooper told Ellen on the phone that afternoon, "this country makes it easy to drop out of sight. Piece of cake the first few months, easy to go total incognito. But for a total fact I have to tell you to stay permanently missing in the U.S., ma'am— what with the network we've developed—a person's got to be a total genius."

The idea that their mother might have disappeared on purpose was put forward by authorities who, after all, had more experience in matters such as this and had to ask the difficult but necessary questions that the situation called for. Was she in financial trouble? Did she seem depressed? Had she been behaving strangely in the weeks preceding what was now referred to as The Incident? Was it likely there was something she was hiding from her daughters? Had she ever traveled outside the U.S.? Had she ever visited inside the iron curtain? What about the commie bloc? How 'bout South America? Was she on some drugs? Did she have a lover? Had their father (twenty years deceased) been black? Did they think their mother was a lesbian?

When Walther the Weimaraner proved in fact not to be Winston the Pekingese and no one around the Denver airport had reported having seen or talked to anyone corresponding to Nina's description, Ellen thought she heard a new note enter the polite response she was getting from the Colorado state troopers. For one thing, apart from the more anxious phone calls that they made to one another, around noon of the second day Pat's, Myra's and Ellen's phones went dead. No one called them. Panic, which was not Pat's or Ellen's element, set in and Myra's early fears of an act of terrorism seemed, in retrospect, entirely quaint. Among them they repeated four words as a fugue, a mounting roundelay in dissonance, a Doppler shift from "Have *you* heard anything?" to "Have you *heard* anything?" until finally, by the evening of the second day, the question was, "Have you heard *anything?*" Meanwhile the storm raged over the Midwest and headed east. Denver Airport closed indefinitely. La Guardia delayed all flights six hours owing to increasing sleet. It was a windless storm, so far as blizzards go—its danger was delivery of a massive snow. There were twenty inches of it fallen in six hours in Nebraska. Roads and runways couldn't be kept clear. In whole parts of the country phone lines had been down since the preceding day. Motorists were cautioned not to drive. On the second night of Nina's disappearance television broadcasters as far east as New York City were advising elderly people to stay at home. Tuning in at random, hearing this, Ellen had her first real grief. She'd had so much to do, she hadn't stopped to think of Nina as *her mother*, as a person. She thought of Nina as somebody out there, a dotty actress in a Hitchcock movie whose disappearance is the basis of a light romantic comedy. She thought of Nina being lost, perhaps completely fuddled, painfully intractable about that stupid ugly dog of hers, but on the move, *moving*, if not in a straight line, moving, nonetheless, with purpose. She hadn't thought of Nina being old, Nina being stopped by weather. Nina being halt. Nina being silenced by forgetfulness, by quarter-mile-long treks to boarding gates, Nina as a nuisance in a fast lane, Nina faltering.

When the phone rang after midnight Ellen jumped at it. It was Colorado trooper Larsen speaking. "We've retrieved a piece of that blue luggage with your mother's name and address on it," he reported in his detailed manner. "We retrieved it from a trash bin in the Denver train station. We've sent it to Forensics for some answers but there's one thing I can tell you with all certainty, without a doubt. The inside of that suitcase was a total empty. Total. Do you hear me, ma'am?"

It takes four hours to fly across the U.S.A. by plane, four days to make the trip by train and maniacs have claimed it can be done by car in less than fifty hours. In the snow nobody moves that fast. The airports close, their runways turn into sleek tundras, railbeds fill like hourglasses, glaciers mass on intercontinental roadway systems. Silence is a symptom of extremes in weather—it's the product of extinction. When the world was young colossi roamed it till extremes began, the dinosaur fell victim to a frozen evolution, stopped before it might have managed to adapt, while earth's more modern creature lasted out bad weather by retreating to its caves. Three days went by.

The snow moved on to Ohio, Pennsylvania and New York. In Massachusetts, Pat waited by her telephone and watched the sky descend. Ellen reported from New York that the storm had hit Long Island with winds of sixty knots and waves at Montauk Point that crested thirty-seven feet. It was expected that the center of the storm would travel northeast on the coast, but it stalled for two days over Nassau County and during those two days Pat felt the atmosphere around her house go heavy. The barometer that hung at the bottom of her stair registered the decline, and the silence grew. No word was heard from Nina. Silence like a baffling snow weighed on all three sisters. There was nothing but this weight where Nina had once been.

Myra acted like she wanted to be blamed. She began to act the Baby. Ellen, oldest, acted equally as juvenile and for the first time in her life wanted to enact a work of violence. When her telephone went dead beneath the storm she tore it out and hit it on the wall until it shattered. Pat, alone, stayed calm. The silence swallowed her. She passed the hours sitting still. When she slept she did it with the telephone nearby, she slept without undressing, ready.

She was sitting with a blanket wrapped around her on a chair beside a fire that had died when Nina called past midnight on the night the snow began to fall in Massachusetts and the call, fulfilling all the odds, arrived collect.

"Patricia—?" Nina said.

"*Mother?* God, where *are* you——?"

"Logal?"

"*What?*"

"A place called 'Logal,' I believe, dear."

"*Logan*, Nina. *Logan.* Are you at Logan, Mother? Boston? Logan. *Are you at the Boston airport, Nina?*"

". . . Pat——?"

". . . Mother——?"

"Pat, I don't know *where* I am."

"You're on the *phone*, keep talking, Nina . . ."

"I'm so tired, dear."

"Is there someone there with you that I can talk to, Nina?"

"Everyone has been so nice. I'm tired. Come and get me, dear."

"I will, but——"

"At this Logal."

"Airport——"

"*Everyone* has been so nice, Patricia."

"Mother, look around. You're calling from a phone booth, right? What's the number? Is there anybody there?"

"There are *lots* of people here, Patricia. This is where they brought us. There's a snowstorm——"

"Yes, I——"

"Winston would have *died.* Do you know, I asked the stewardess. They don't heat that part where dogs are kept."

"*Nina?* Can you read the number of the pay phone to me, please——?"

"I don't have my reading glasses with me, Pat."

"Get them, Mother. I'll hang on."

"I think I must have left them on the bus. Patricia? Don't leave the house, dear, without trying to get through to Ellen. You know how much I worry about her living in New York and now the operator tells me that her phone is out of order."

"Mother, listen, yes, of course, I'll do that, I'll phone Ellen. But can you tell me where you are *exactly?*"

"Logal, dear."

"Are you near an airline counter?"

"Yes, of course, Patricia. Airline counters are the things airports are famous for."

"What airline counters are you near?"

"Eastern, Piedmont, Allegheny—"

"Is there someone there? Behind the counters?"

"There might be, Patricia."

"*Can you see a person at an airline counter, Nina?*"

"Yes."

"Good. *Who?*"

"A woman."

"Good. *Go and tell that woman that I want to talk to her.*"

"Why, Patricia?"

"Go and tell her, Nina. Put the phone down, don't hang up and go and tell her."

Several minutes later Nina picked the phone back up and said, "She says she doesn't want to talk to you, Patricia."

"Tell her it's an emergency."

"She says she's the cleaning lady. Stranded, like the rest of us. I've been wearing the same clothes for *three days,* dear."

"Nina, Jesus Christ, you should have *called*—"

"There aren't telephones on trains. Patricia."

"You've been on a *train?*"

"There aren't telephones on buses, either. And they wouldn't stop to let poor Winston out to take his walk until Ed, my friend. God bless him, went right up and had a word in front of everybody with that driver."

"*—Ed?*"

"God bless him."

" 'Ed'?"

"Yes."

"Who's this 'Ed'?"

"I told you. A very nice kind gentleman."

"Did this 'Ed' get taken to the airport, too?"

"Well, of course. We all did, dear. If it wasn't for 'this

Ed' as you call him, I don't know how I would have managed. I could barely manage Winston what with those two suitcases. I had to leave one suitcase empty when I took the train. Oh, it was frightful, dear. Poor Winston. I never would have managed. There we were in Colorado, just imagine. Me and Winston and two bags, so I emptied one. It was that blue one, dear, that big one that I packed my winter coat in, so I took the coat out and just carried it. Where was that, I have to think. Denver, it might have been—"

"*Nina?* Could you do me a favor? Could you stop and look around a minute and tell me if you see this 'Ed' there in the airport?"

"Well, of course I see him, dear."

"You see him—?"

"Yes."

"Could you get him to come over?"

" 'Over,' Pat?"

"Over to you, please?"

"Well, he's standing right in front of me, Patricia. If you'd ever let him have the chance, he'd like to have a word with you."

Before he closed his eyes he had been telling her about his son, which had come as a surprise, because Nina figured Ed had never married.

She liked to think she could tell when men her age had spent their lives with women, same as she liked to think that she could notice right away if someone near her age had been an army man. Army men know how to make their beds, she'd always told her daughters. Her husband Tom had been a navy man and had seen a lot of action in the China Sea— aside from that he'd learned, like army men, about neat corners, how to square a sheet. All these stories ran together, Nina thought. It seemed you couldn't be her age without one story trailing on another. "*I* was in the army," Ed had told her.

"I could tell," she answered.

"I could speak a bit of Polish back in those days," Ed had said. "They sent me to a displaced persons camp in Germany. You know, to translate. Me, with my Midwestern Polish. Still, I always wanted to go back there, some day. See the town after the war. The way it was in peacetime."

Blah blah blah, she might have thought. Sentimentality ran deep but narrow at their age. "So why didn't you?" she asked.

"Oh, you know, the usual. I'll say this—the army made a man of me."

"Well, I've heard *that* before," she said.

Ed said when things get said a lot they take on their own truth, even when they're false. Then he shocked her when he said, "Like saying 'I love you' or 'I'm too young to die.' "

For a long time Ed just sat there, silent, hardly moving but to nuzzle Winston, leaving Nina with the job of talking, which was why she thought he'd been a single gentleman, because it seemed he wasn't used to conversation. "You feel all right, Ed?" she was more than once provoked to ask.

He apologized and said that he was very tired.

"Me too," Nina said.

"How long have you been traveling?" she asked, following another silence.

"Couple days."

"And where're you from?"

"St. Louis. Everybody nowadays says, 'Outside St. Louis,' though, I've noticed. As a city it died twenty, thirty years ago. The town's extinct. . . ."

"So you're on vacation?" Nina asked.

"Oh, at our age, sure. Life's a permanent vacation."

"I'm on a visit to my daughter," Nina said. "Where're you going?"

"If I tell you, you'll die laughing."

She looked at him expectantly.

"Is it somewhere funny?"

"You might say so, sure."

"Plymouth Rock?" she guessed.

"Why do you say that?" Ed asked.

"Well, because Plymouth Rock is funny."

"Plymouth Rock is?"

"Funny. Yes. Have you ever been there?"

"No."

"Well," Nina said, as if she'd proved a point. "You should go someday. You'd see."

"I've seen its picture. In 'The Rock' commercials."

"In 'The Rock'?"

"You know. 'Own a piece.' Insurance."

"That's Gibraltar."

"That's Gibraltar—?"

"Yes."

"But Gibraltar isn't in America."

"Well, no, but not too many people know that, Ed."

"Well, that's not right. That's not right at all. They ought to use a native rock for that. One of our own. They ought to use the Plymouth Rock for that."

"Well, that's what I was saying, see. They couldn't."

"Why not?"

"Because it's small."

"It's small?"

Ed was looking down at Winston so Nina said, "Not that all small things are funny, Ed, but what they've done to Plymouth Rock is, they've built a cage around it. It's so people won't deface it, you know, with their names and dates. They've built this big cage 'round this tiny thing. Patricia—she's the one who's coming out to pick me up, the one you talked to on the phone—Patricia, she was always serious, full of questions that were hard to answer, you know how children are. Full of questions. I took Patricia there to

Plymouth Rock when she was young and she had to stand up on her toes to look at it through the cage, this tiny thing inside a big enclosure, and she said, real loud, mind you, so everyone could hear, 'Will it come out at feeding time, Mommy?' "

Nina laughed at her own reminiscence but Ed looked hard put to respond appropriately and Nina realized she had changed the subject to herself again, to her past, the way her daughters said she always did these days, and she felt embarrassed for herself. Ed was such a nice man. She should learn to talk to people better, take an interest in the things that they began to tell her. When he'd been quiet several minutes and she found the silence unsupportable, she offered him a mint, which he refused, so she took two for herself. Then she cleared her throat and said, "Do you have any hobbies, Ed?" and that's when he began to talk about his son. He said he hadn't had a hobby since his son was just a boy. He didn't know, exactly, where his son was now. They used to make scale models of the dinosaurs together.

Nina focused all her interest on the story and said, "Oh?", but Ed fell into another silence, so she asked him, "When was that?"

"Oh, you know," he said. "Forty years ago, I guess. Maybe it was fifty."

He asked her if she'd mind if he took a little nap even though he'd promised Pat he'd keep an eye on her, and Nina answered, "No, go right ahead," but when he'd been asleep about ten minutes he suddenly sat up and looked at her and said, "What was that name of that most famous one, I can't remember."

Nina thought she must have dozed off, too, because she couldn't understand what he was saying.

" 'Famous'?" she asked.

"The famous one, the one the other dinosaurs were afraid of," Ed explained.

Nina frowned and said, "I'm not too smart in this department, Ed, my girls all ran a detour 'round that age when children are preoccupied with things like snakes and dinosaurs."

"It was something with two names," Ed told her.

" 'Two names'? Well, there were those monsters, at the time," Nina answered feebly, "in the movies. Big ones. King Kong and the like. He had two names—"

"I know it wasn't *bronto*sauras," Ed continued, "it was something else. Two names. Walked on its hind legs. It was the biggest one. . . ."

He looked at Nina and she saw that he looked very tired, so she touched him lightly on his hand. To her surprise the gesture sparked a darkened corner of her memory because she heard herself recite the word, "Tyrannosaurus."

Ed squeezed her hand.

"That's a girl!" she heard him saying. He was grinning ear to ear. "What a girl!" he marveled. " 'Tyrannosaurus,' yes, 'tyrannosaurus'!" he repeated, " 'tyrannosaurus-*something*' . . . well, I'm happy now. I bet you thought we'd both forgotten. . . ."

She wanted to inquire what he meant by "two names," but he closed his eyes and looked like he was sleeping so she waited, then she started feeling sleepy, too, and then she just forgot the question. The next thing that she knew someone was pulling on her shoulder and she woke and saw Pat's face. It was dark outside. She could see the dark behind Pat's face, outside the big glass windows. She woke slowly, feeling very tired. Slowly she began to realize she had fallen against Ed, gone to sleep against his shoulder with her winter coat around the two of them. Hours must have passed. She saw that Pat looked worried.

"Was the driving that bad, dear?" Nina asked, but Pat answered with another question.

"Mother, is this Ed?" she asked.

She made an angry movement with her foot on Winston's back which Nina didn't like at all and then she gave him a sharp rap above the eyes so he'd keep still.

"*Patricia!*" Nina whispered. "What's got into you—?"

"Answer, Nina," Pat said in a strange, tight way. "Is this Ed?"

"—not so loud, you'll wake him, let the poor man sleep, Patricia. What's the matter with you, why are you being nasty with poor Winston—?"

Pat touched Nina on her cheek and Nina blinked.

Cold was coming from somewhere. Cold was coming from beneath her coat. Pat was asking her another question. What's she asking *this* time? Nina wondered. It seemed she'd spent her whole life answering these questions. Why don't people on the South Pole fall from Earth? How many days till Christmas? Why do Pat and Ellen have blue eyes like Daddy and I don't? Why does Myra have her own room? Why is that person wearing that? Why are his hands so blue? Did he say where he was going, Nina? Mother? Did he tell you his last name?

LONDON
NOVEMBER 1987

151

SHIBBOLETBOO

WELL YORE NOT GONE BELIEBE THIS, but that tabacca monkey Ray wuz wif her at her deaf, an' halfway through the best part ub the sugareats he stand up an' claim like some accusted jay, "Yuz all shud hear whut Miz Boo had t' say last thing. Miz Boo's dyin' wuds," he sez. "She look t' me an' say, 'Ray?' She say, 'Ray? Why is men behabe so nast—?' "

Well I'll tell you, that tabacca monkey cud hab tunned into a monkey true in front ub us an' nuffin' wud hab shocked us more'n whut he'd sayd. I mean, my pie stuck t' my teef. Neber heard such lies afore from no one wuzint planderin' my bote or honeyin' some money off ub me. *Miz Boo's dyin' wuds*, my ars'n'l—it wuz like the partin' ub the Red Sea 'round that monkey after that. Mind you, Mister Ray has neber been no Moses so people moobed away an' left him wide alone. 'Cept batty Missus Olly. She goes up an' shake her face in Ray's. "Slanderin' the dead!" she sez. "Eb'rybody knows Miz Boo wuz cut out from her tongue at birf. Dumb as diapers! Eb'rybody knows it. So hesh up! Filf don't seed no miracles on earf."

Well all the belfries in the county hain't as dingy as Missus Olly is, but fo' one'st she rang a li'l true. Bein' dead wuz not the reason Miz Boo had gone silence like a stone— she wuz mutified afore she lapsed. Long afore, if maybe not, as Missus Olly assertained, from birf. I, nor any other pusson, 'ceptin' Ray, cudint recollect ub hearin' anyfin' Miz Boo had need t' say an' that's the troof.

Well but Ray's so orn'ry he stand there an' repeats hisself like indibidal bolls lined in a cotton field. "I think yuz all shud know her dyin' wuds," he sez. "She look t' me an' sez, she sez, 'Ray? *Why* is men so nast?' " Then he sit down.

Well Missus Olly's standin' there an' she sez, "I hain't neber heard such load ub cowdunk in my life," an' I think she spoke fo' allub us. I mean, whut's Ray mean by actin' "nast"? Whut's "nast" mean I'd like t' know. Is we supposed t' think Miz Boo ran short ub breaf there at the end too pooped by the excitin' miracle ub speech t' breave the final eee in nasty? I mean, I wud truly like t' know whut we're supposed t' think. Eb'ry miracle has meanin', I beliebe. Otherwise, it's just another self-misplained phenomenon like flyin' shoes.

Well so yude think Ray wud hab had his full ub stimulatin' negatibity but up he pop again like someone's annibersary an' sez, "An' futhermore, the men she wuz referrin' t' is sittin' right here at this inhumation," an' he points, usin' those two mutilated digitals ub his cut off wif Mister Wendell's whippymaker.

Well I mean, "inhumation"? Makes you wonder how some people get theys talk. Custed eban-Jell-o's are the cause I reckon. Eber listen t' that spout ub holy moly on the radio? Cain't call toleratin' others plain ol' toleratin', hab t' call it Milk ub Christian Kindness. Hain't satisfied in callin' dyin' dyin', hab t' call it Summoned By The Lord. A pusson duzint die no more, that pusson Ascends Into God's Eternal Temple. 'Course, talk hab always been grand-eloquent wif eban-gelatins but now you get your ab'rage used car salesman patternin' hisself from eban-jellyrolls, 'stead ub how they used t' hero wuship tricky dick. It's in the wuds themselfs these days, I think, pollution ub the darkest kine. Otherwise how wud some tabacca monkey plain-ub-brain as Ray recite a wud like "inhumation" 'cept from inhalation ub some mutant syllables from KGOD Radio or from committin' cathode escesses wif Christian channels on the cable? I mean, we weren't at any "inhumation," we wuz at the inhumation *party*, those who had inhumated the deceased habing done so earlier an' those who had not, they'd come around t' join the rumination ub some sugareats an' pie laid on by Major an' The Spinster, in respect ub their dead sister. So there we wuz, when t' eb'rybody's malcontent duzint Ray pop up an' point his stubbun witch's nubbles on them, sayin', "Futhermore, the men she wuz referrin' t' is sittin' right here at this inhumation."

Well The Major an' The Spinster hain't esactly "men," you know, not in the strictest sense cud anybody point at them an' ast, "Why is *men* behabe so nast?," but that wuz why Ray's accusation wuz sulfuriously snickered at. The Spinster is as unlike any woman as your ab'rage weebil. Fact, that's whut people call her, as you know, owin' t' her snout. Kine you use t' pry the lid off cans. Plus she still retains whut people call her "girlish skin." Kine whut neber obercame its acme.

Well so that's The Spinster an' I don't need t' tell you whut The Major made his Major in.

Well there we wuz, about the entire population ub the town, 'cept fo' Hen an' Billy Marshall who wuz ober t' Prince George fo' the other fun'ral. Bunn me if it don't most often wuk that way that you can go fo' months wif no fun'ral t' attend an' then two people up an' die at one'st in two separate counties. I wuz nearly goin' t' go wif Bill an' Hen but then I got t' thinkin' how it wuz Miz Boo arribed at bein' called that name an' dang if I cud hafway recollect. So I baked a pecan pie an' sent it on wif Hen an' Bill an' skipped the inhumation (cannot tolerate the dust, whut wif all my asthma) an' took myself on ober to The Spinster's an' The Major's house fo' sugareats an' gen'ral infomation. Well whut are inhumation parties fo'? I was gone t' ask The Spinster how we started callin' Boo that name cuz cust me, I just cudint recollect. I mean, I cud remember her real name clear, remember sittin' in the schoolroom while Miz Jackson called on Nancy t' recite. "Come on, Nancy," Miz Jackson wud insist, "eb'ry-body knows it can be done if you just try." "She needs a *miracle*," The Major, who back then wuz known as Jimmy Junior, wud poke fun. "She's *dumb*," The Spinster wud rem-ine us all as if we all wuz needin' a remine. "Might as well try Bear t' make a speech," The Spinster said. Bear, as you re-member, wuz our Main Street mongrel. Eb'ryone's an' no body's. Spinster's name back then wuz Lorelei. Lovely Lorelei, remember? How can such a pretty girl result so ugly, I wud like t' know. Some inner sourability, I reckon. Gunk in place ub honey.

Well so I wuz gone t' ask the former siren how her sister got her name but fust out ub politeness I wuz sittin' down wif Arthuritic Richards fo' some lemon pie. When Ray stand up like he wuz de-possessed ub nat'ral quiet an' points ac-cusin' stubs at Major and The Spinster.

Well you know The Major is a mass ub man. You know that look he gets. You know when his eyelids seem t' shut from some enormous weight like pennies pressed agin' them fo' the ferryman. Well he got that look. Then he sez to Ray, "*Suh*. You are speakin' in owwa hawse. You are speakin' ub owwa dear departed sistah, suh. May I remine."

Well it seems you cain't go t' any inhumation party these days wifout it tunns into an alligator wrassle. Too many people learnin' how t' act from watchin' people try an' talk t' one another on TB is whut I see t' blame. I mean, you see it on C-Span. You see it all the time on daytime TB lady host-ess shows. Loudmoufed an' opinurated. Uncouf an' obeast. So Ray sez, "You think Miz Boo hain't tol' me whut you twos hab done when yous wuz children? If dat whut you think den yous dummer den you eber made yore sistah out t' be."

Well talk about some firewuks, I don't know which esploded louder, Major or Nebada Flats. The Major might hab been some kine ub secrit army weapon all hisself. Get out ub my hawse. You second-rate intelligence. No one in this town has eber liked you. I'll make sutain you won't wuk agin. When I'm done wif helpin' people know the troof on you, you won't hab courage t' subibe the spot yore libbin' in. You uppity unprintable. I'll rune you. Yule rue the day you dared accuse The Major an' et cetera.

Well it wuz thrillin' for us all t' tell the troof. Threats an' accusations just like ol' Nikita, just like ol' Miz Jackson, just like on "The Simpsons," oh The Major wuz real hot. Eb'ry-body thought that Ray wud cower an' renounce hisself but he just stood his groun' an' kept repeatin' the ridiculous, i.e., "*Why* is men behabe so nast?" like it wuz keepin' him alibe an' breavin' 'til The Major leabes the room an' comes back wif his rifle an' discharges two shells at poor ol' Ray's poor monkey's pod.

Well I'm happy t' report Ray didint sacrifice his life on principle 'cuz fo' reasons later provin' t' esempt The Major from due process ub the Law, the shot in those two shells wuz potent as ol' Arthuritic Richards so the damage done wuz nuffin' more'n gen'ral panic.

Well I bet yore sorried you weren't there, though more total waste ub sugareats I cain't remember. Things took a nast tunn soon's The Major manifested his artillerary—folks all picked up in a hurry after that, haf-eaten lemon pie an' all. Neber did obtain the opp'tunity t' question Spinster Lorelei on how her sister gots her name when duzintit occur t' me t' gib that Ray ridehome in my chevy. "If it's all the same t'you," he sez, "I'll go as far as t' the cementary. Want t' sit a while, conberse there wif Miz Boo."

"Well now Ray," I sez, "the dead are singularly trust-worvy fo' keepin' theys moufs shut." He shrug. Fo' a man who wuz most recently near dead hisself, he seem distinctly cool. "Oh Miz Boo an' me, we telepaff," he sez. "That right?" I ast.

"Well then," I sez, "How wud you think ub passin' on a question that's been naggin' on my mine, from me t' her? Along wif my commiserates, ub course."

"Well dat depens," Ray sez. "I hain't but neber telepaffed wif her since she be dine."

Well nest thing whut I knows we standin' at the new dug grabe an' I cain't keep myself from sayin' in disgust, "Cheapstates." "Ma'am?" Ray ast.

"Well I neber," I reiterates. "Yude think with all the welf The Major gots he might not skint on sumpin' everlas-tin' as a stone. I mean," I sez. I point t' where there isn't but a single wud on her memorial. "Man owns a chizlin' repu-tation his whole life 'til the one occasion when some chizlin' counts, then he skints. Yude think The Spinster and The Major might hab plentished up some scroll-de-roll, some 'R.I.P.', some 'Here Lies Our Belubbed Sister,' some 'Unto Your Eternal Heaben, Lord' in place ub this pathetic insult, 'nuff t' scare the hair off necromancers. 'B O O.' Whut kine ub thing is that? Some stranger gone come along some cen-tury from now an' see this as some kine ub joke. 'B O O.' I neber. On a toomstone. In a cementary, eben."

"Well it's whut she wanted."

"Well I'm sorry I just think it's crude."

"Well wuz her own dyin' wish."

"Well someone ought t' made her change her mine. 'B O O.' I tell you, Ray, it is disgraceful. It's one thing on a Halloween, you know, or in a comic book somewhere, comin' from a friendly ghost like Caspar—playin' hide an' seek or sumpin', friendly scary games—but this is pure hu-milifyin' t' the other pussons buried here aroun' . . ."

"Well but all theys other pussons daid."

"Well so *whut*? You mean you think the daid do not enjoin some common cut'essy?"

"Well no."

"Well sorry, Ray. Yore wrong."

"Well I'm sorry, too. Mean, they's *daid*, ma'am. We don't hab t' act cut'ious t' them just cuz they's *daid*, is whut I mean. Not if we wuzn't cut'ious t' them in theys life. Just 'cuz a pusson's daid I don't beliebe that mean we owe 'em sumpin' that we neber showed when they wuz libbin'. Bein' daid don't mean we has t' forstake who they wuz."

"Well where's the 'wuz' ub this here woman, then? Where's the dates ub her particulars? When wuz she birfed? Who wuz her forebears? Whut's her fam'bly name? People gone come here years along an' wonder, '*Huh*—?' I mean . . . do you understand me, Ray . . . people will take one stunned look at this an' murmur, '*Huh*?' Who the hell wuz this? Duz-int eben say if it wuz man or woman—just sez this one ol' stupid frighty wud. Duzint eben gib a clue t' who she *wuz*."

"Well she wuz Boo. That's all she wuz."

Well I can tell you I wuz ready t' desutt the monkey 'cept fo' then an' there, I swear, it must ub been the cementary an' my wholly earnest distaste ub such places, but, you won't beliebe this, while I stand there it come back t' me. The burried past. Maybe it wuz Ray, whut Ray said, "She wuz Boo, that's all she wuz," but sumpin' gabe away just then, like those tectonic plates burried undergroun', but on a smaller scale, natch, not like the moon ejectin' ub itself from the Pacific—some kine ub smaller catyclism, bein' sumpin' inside me an' not inside the his'try ub the earf:

Sheboo noboo liboo uboo.

Ignoboo heboo.

Iboo weboo caboo ignoboo heboo,
Weboo caboo kilboo heboo.

Well, well. I spelunked the well ub mem'ry wifout hyp-
nosis nor a miracle from Christ, boaf ub which are put at my
disposal, fo' a small donation, on TB. Just standin' there, it
all come back t' me. I mean, I one'st listened t' a all night
program the whole night, cuz it wuz so fascinatin', where a
campaign manager fo' a mid-West politician an' a economist
wuz talkin' t' the minister whose show it wuz about how
much the ministry ub Christ wud cost today if Christ shows
up tomorra. An' it wuz fascinatin' stuff. Airline trabel, libe
(or re-alibe) on satellite TB. The minister wuz sure that
Christ wud only go t' Christian countries but no one said,
"Well, that will sabe a lot ub money." An' it will keep Him
far away from where He libbed His fust time 'round, nobody
bovvered t' point out. Maybe if I told this t' a TB minister,
if I told him how my mem'ry re-stored itself standin' in the
cementary, he wud tell me Jesus did it. Maybe he wud start
t' pray an' thank the Lord fo' me. He wud not esclude me
from his prayers at any rate, this I know cuz I see these men,
these ministers, on telebision an' they seem real nice. They
do not, as Boo wud put it, act so nast. Only, in that prayin',
don't we know, there might be wuds that's said, some two
or three, a dozen wuds, that only followers can understand,
only the insiders, people who's a member ub the tribe already: that's how Lorelei an' Jimmy Junior made their sister
Nancy into B O O. I saw it standin' there aside ub Ray,
recubberin' my mem'ry from that single wud. Ray wuz
telepaffin', seemed t' me—such things is hard t' know wifout
esperience. Maybe he wuz merely prayin'. Anyway, his eyes
wuz closed. It's easy, see. It started as a game, at fust. You
hab t' be like us, you see? You take a wud. You take a wud,
see, an' you drop its final consinent. You know how t' recognize those consinents. Those letters whuts not bowels.

Drop the final consinent—replace it wif a *boo*. HATE becomes hā*boo*. LOVE becomes lo*boo*—but so duz LONE an' LOT an' LOW an' LOSE an' LOCO—all ub them becomes lo*boo*, so it gets confusin' when yore just startin' out. Fo' a wud whut duzint hab a consinent you add a *boo* there on the end. So ME becomes me*boo*. But so does MEN. An' MET an' MEDIA, MESA an' MENU. As you can see, it's not a language ub precision. It requires intuition. It requires learnin' plain talk fust. But from the time their mother, rest her bones, delibbered them their sister, Lorelei an' Jimmy undertook t' speak esclusibly in *boo*. *You hab t' be like us t' understand us*, their message wuz. An' they cud speak it fast. It made the rest ub us try hard at fust t' play along wif them but in the end it made us sick an' tired. Fact wuz, I remember one day I discubbered that the only wud that wuz the same between the language that we spoke an' their inbented language wuz the wud *taboo*. TABOO wuz *taboo* in boaf our languages. TABOO wuz *taboo* in Lorelei's an' Jimmy's *boo*-talk—but *taboo* in *boo*-talk wuz the wud fo' TAKE an' TAME an' TALE an' TAG an' TAPE an' TAR an' TAP an' TAX, as well. It wuz eshaustin', tryin' t' keep up wif them fo' those ub us who hafway understood—it wuz impossible fo' Nancy. From the fust she started talkin', she followed 'long behind her brother an' her sister goin' boo boo boo boo thinkin' she wuz makin' sense. It wuz pathetic. Meanwhile Lorelei an' Jimmy haf *gooboo morninboo*ed an' *gooboo nighboo*ed eb'ryone t' deaf. It grew disgustin'. They talked so fast. *Helboo*, they'd start t' parrot at anyone who'd listen, *hoboo aboo youboo toboo*? That's, "Hello, how are you today?"

Not well. Nancy followed them around an' didint seem t' want t' learn t' talk t' no one else. The only thing she wanted wuz t' talk like them, belong t' them, t' be included, not escluded, in their language. As I say, the rest ub us got downright sick an' tired ub it afterwhile an' went on talkin' on our own in our own language. An' eb'rytime Jimmy an' that Lorelei had t' answer sumpin' in the schoolroom? t' Miz Jackson? had t' ast fo' sumpin' at the store? or sabe their libes? They neber used that *boo*-talk. Neber one'st. Only front ub Nancy. Now that I remember it, I hab t' think it wuz a crime the way they *boo*ed that chile. They *boo*ed that chile to deaf.

"Well Ray?" I fine'ly ast ub him. He duzint moob. "Is you finish wif yore conbersation?" He just stand. You eber seen them dowsers? Crazy people walkin' roun' wif branches from a tree in search ub fountains undergroun'?

Well Ray remine me ub them. Stuck his arms out ober Miz Boo's grabe. Saw him in my rear-biew mirra as I drobe away. Looked just like some rig there, silhouetted, Texas-style. Drillin' at some well ub silence.

WILLIAMSBURG, VIRGINIA
AUGUST 1990

BIO SLEPCU

In Prague, during Kafka's lifetime,
there was a movie house called Bio Slepcu.
Its name means Cinema for the Blind.

YOU WOULDN'T THINK, to look at her, that she was
going through what she was going through. She looked a
little puffy-faced, that's all, a little imprecise across the cheek-
bones, face looked kind of slept-in, like a rumpled bed,
around her eyes. Could have been she was hung over or a
user, but he knew she wasn't like that. Didn't used to be, at
least. No, too much salt and sugar, glass too many of a
mediocre European wine, sinus problem, maybe, or her time
of month, that's the way she looked. Lots of people look that
way when they wake up. She looked like she had woken up
from sleeping in an airtight room. Never fucking. Eating
beef. What the fuck kinda hazards in the world these days.
Anything could do it.

So he let his eyes graze down her body. Well, this
woman. Still all there. Luther used to be in love with her.
Sometimes in a lonely moment he remembered. Little things.
The way she used to get goose bumps. She used to get goose
bumps on her thighs, along the sides, when she was sexually

excited. Aren't too many women's thighs who act like that.
Not that Luther knew. Another thing, she bruised too easy.
She had this thing for going purple at a touch. Something
simple, like a knock into the coffee table, made her come up
looking like she'd ridden sidecar with Kit Carson on a bronco
bust from Wichita to Amarillo. Maybe that was what they
call an early warning. A symptom, all that bruising. Maybe,
even then, there was something doing dirty in her blood.
Luther was immune to maybes. He had had the shits of
them. Maybe this and maybe that. Maybe if and only maybe.
Hey was she so pure? She had roughed him up on her part,
roughed him up real bad. He had bruises, in and out. Any
two combatants in a marriage come equipped for heavy war-
fare. Luther knew it. Luther had seen action. Hit the ground
and shat himself but Luther kept on running. "Tough guy,"
now she says. It was what she called him. Like the first thing
in those moments after love. Like just about the time his
thing went turkey fat inside her. "So what's all this?" he says.
She was wearing like a one-piece, dress, that showed her
legs. "You can take your hat off," she tells Luther. So okay
the truth was he had lost some hair and had some new stuff
planted. "Christ," she says, "that must have hurt." Her fingers almost want to touch it. That's the point at which she
smiles and lays the tough guy on him.

Well hey the woman always had that smile. Great legs
and that great smile. Take a seat, she tells him. Luther looks
around and doesn't see a thing that looks familiar. Except for
her. "All new stuff," he recognizes. He sits down and the
chair feels small for him. Wonders if she meant for him to sit
beside her on the sofa. "Nice," he says. "Place shows some
taste." Oh yeah this is your first time here, she says. Like it's
such a dumbfuck kinda thing to say she must be nervous.
"Hey Marie you nervous?" Luther says.

"I'm scared," she says and Luther isn't ready for it.

"So this thing is gonna cost a lotta money, huh?" he
says. "I hope you kept that policy I bought ya."

"Yeah I kept the policy," she says. "You want a drink?"

"Sure." Anything to change the subject. "What ya got?"

"I got your favorite," and she goes into the kitchen. Two years since I've seen this woman, Luther thinks, I've had a lotta favorites. "Rolling Rock," she says and hands him one. "Oh yeah," he says and he remembers. Tinny-tasting beer. While what he wants right now is scotch.

"So Marie," he says, "make sure they hold your job, you know? Don't take no shit, there's laws these days."

"Well sure," she says. She's drinking sparkling water. "But first things first."

Luther pours the beer into the glass she brought and then despite himself he folds the can inside his hand, he can't believe it. Then he pulls another asinine maneuver, puts the fucking thing inside his jacket pocket.

"First I have to get through this," Marie is saying. Luther drinks. "Sure," he says, "that's obvious." He thinks perhaps he isn't being cool.

"So like, what," he says, "I mean. Do you need money? I mean, if you need money, you know. I don't have it."

For the first time since he's walked in Luther takes the time to really look at her. Probably because she's sitting still. Probably because she's looking back at him. "Did I ever take your money, tough guy?" she asks quietly.

"Not so far," he says.

She opens out her hands, palms up, and shrugs.

"So what's the deal, Marie," he says.

"Nothing."

" 'Nothing.' I mean. You tell me on the phone you need to talk to me in person."

"Yes."

"So here I am. In person."

"So it seems."

"So the fuck it seems? What am I, see through?"

Big round eyes, her other weapon. Turn her big round eyes on you. "Look," he says, "you sure it isn't money?"

"It's not money, Luther."

"So what is it, then. I mean. There's not a lot that I can do. You know I don't go visit at no hospitals. You need someone to go with you, is that it? I can fix a cab."

"There's no one else I have to talk to about this."

"Well why is that?"

"Why do you think?"

"And anyway. I'm not a doctor."

"Well I thought, you know. A little comfort."

This was a mistake, he thinks. Looks around and sees the exit. Looks again at his ex-wife.

"What is that supposed to mean?" he asks.

"Comfort," she repeats.

"What kinda comfort?"

"What kind have you got?"

"Not the kind you have in mind, Marie."

"What kind is that?"

"Look," he says. Stands up. "I'm sorry you don't have some guy. All right? Two years now, it's not my fault."

Marie sits there.

"They make hair in test tubes now," she says. "They know how to make it grow." She turns those big eyes on him. "Read it in this morning's paper." She stands up. Turns that big smile on him, too. "So you should have waited, Luther. Before going through . . ." She waves her fingers toward his hair.

"I'm sure glad you're here to tell me what I should have done, Marie," he answers and he puts his hat back on. All the times he's bragged about the way she can't get over him. Women don't get over me, he brags to all the guys. I mean, my wife. No other guy for two whole years. It's starting, you know, what they say. To be pathetic.

They are standing in her hallway by the door.

"Well this was shit, thank you," she says.

He doesn't want to stand that close to her so he steps

back, thinks about his exit line. "So what they do," he says. Out of politeness. "They go in and take it out, or what?"

"They take it out."

"They tell you, like, beforehand?"

"Tell me what?"

"How much they're gonna take."

She makes that palm-up shrug again.

"Well," he says. He is ready, now, to go. "If it's any consolation to you. Just remember it's a common thing. You ain't the first."

He can tell she's going to kiss him, so he moves his right foot in that way he's learned to do, his right foot a full step ahead to turn his thigh against the woman, sideways, so she won't notice his limp thing. Full front, standing, gives it all away so he had learned this little trick, a quarter twist. If he's sitting in a car with them, or on their sofa, he can cross his legs. Keep the patter up and go on petting. Tell them how you want to get to know them as a person first before you fuck them and they think you are the best news since the Pill, a fucking walking condom-covered nice-guy with a heart of gold, until you never call again or go around to see them, duck their calls. Two years and the thing he tells himself that he will never do is he will never try and stimulate it, you know, on his own. Okay so he has this problem since he's left Marie. So lots of guys can't get it up so what. But a man who masturbates is someone saying he's alone. Luther isn't saying he's alone. So many women, christ, and he wants to fuck them all, the way they taste, the way each one is slightly different, some who cry out like to have their titties sucked, and young ones bored and perfect, yes, he likes them best because they let him go through all the motions and they never noticed. Blind, that's what he robs them like, he robs them blind, of bits of selves they thought they could dispose of here and there, a loveless kiss, the loveless exhibition, loveless touching, loveless promise, loveless love. This woman now, this woman that he used to love, Marie, she was the last thing on the planet that he wished to touch because she knew too much, they'd gone together out of love and into what the fuck this kinda shit and there was nothing he could do to comfort her and there was nothing that her body held for him that offered any promise of desire, any hope or any change. Still she pressed against him but the way she kissed him was without a spark and it was almost careful. It was not unpleasant but it wasn't pleasing either. Slowly, then, she moved her hands up to his chest and felt inside his jacket. He liked to have his nipples touched and only she, of all the women for two years, knew how to do that, and she seemed to know, too, right away, that there was nothing in it now, that something dark had fallen on them where there once was light, she moved her hands away and put them at his wrists and brought his fists up to her own breasts, pried his fingers open, held them on her flesh and he could feel her nipples harden at his palms and then, beneath his left one, he could feel that other hardness, round, inside the soft globe of her breast. Like a blaze of dawn but—how to say this— unseen, like a blind man in a cinema, he began to have a vision of a thing he couldn't see. He hadn't even asked her which breast was it but he could feel it, now, between his fingers, holding it within her flesh, it shocked him and it thrilled him, thrilled him for the first time in two years, he could see it with his fingers, hard seed of a living death, like something, like some rock of gold or jet or amethyst, graven image of my god a nut a trigger, he could see the whole thing that it was, he put his head against her breast and she said Luther I've got goose bumps. Marie, let me, he thought he said. Marie. Don't cry. Instead.

LONDON
NOVEMBER 1990

GROCER'S DAUGHTER

I AM SHAMELESS in the way I love my father.

Like little girls who ride big horses, big girls who hold their fathers in devotion are talked about in overtones of sexual pathology. Love is always judged. No one's love is like another's. What I feel is mine, alone. If my heart is in my mouth, and if I speak it, judgment comes. Surviving judgment, like admitting love, takes courage. Here is what John Wiggins taught me:

The moon at crescent is God's fingernail.

When your shelves look empty, stack your canned goods toward the front.

Keep your feet off other people's furniture.

Don't lean your belly on the scale weighing out the produce, or the Devil will tip it his way when your time comes.

Take anybody's check.

Go nowhere in a hurry.

Sing.

Take your hat off inside churches and in the rain, when the spirit moves you.

Don't wax cucumbers.

Don't sleep late on Sundays.

Start each week with gratitude and six clean aprons.

He was born in Pennsylvania, died in the woods and never, to my knowledge, saw an island. He sunburned easily. He wore a yellow pencil stub behind his ear for jotting orders. He was so accustomed to jotting grocery orders on a pad for a clerk to read, he lost his longhand. The supermarkets in the suburbs squeezed him out. We moved a lot. Each time we moved, the house got smaller, things we didn't need got sold. We didn't need his army helmet or the cardboard notebooks, black and white, in which he'd learned to write. One can't save everything. One trims the fat, one trims the lettuce: produce, when it comes in crates from Florida, needs trimming. For years I saved the only letter he'd written in his lifetime to me. He'd printed it, of course, so there'd be no misunderstanding in the way a pen can curve a word. I lost that letter in my latest move. It's said three moves are like a single fire in their power to destroy one's camp. We moved nine times before I was eighteen. I search in vain, sometimes, for anything my father might have touched.

He always liked a good laugh; his jokes weren't always funny. He concocted odd pranks. He scared my mother half to death one year, when they were first married, by burglarizing their apartment. He rigged a water bucket on his sister's bedroom door the night of her first date: that was 1939, when cotton dresses took half an hour's pressing and a girl might spend an afternoon wrapping dark hair on a curling iron. To my mother, who gets dizzy looking in round mirrors, he wrote love letters that germinated from the center of the page and spiraled out. Those days, he still wrote in script. I think I could identify his longhand, if need be. Handwriting speaks. I think I could remember his.

I remember what his footsteps sounded like: heavier on one leg than the other, made the change rattle in his pocket. He always carried change, most grocers did, because the kids would come in to buy cookies from the bin with pennies and their pennies crowded up the cash drawer. Year in, year out, he wore pleated pants in dark colors. He had three good suits—one gray, one black, one brown. I see him in them in the photographs. The gray one took a lot of coaxing from my mother and wasn't often worn. Every year for Christmas he received:

> six new pairs of black socks
> six new undershirts
> six pairs of boxer shorts
> two new sweater vests
> six white shirts
> six aprons
> one subdued pastel shirt from me
> one knit tie from my sister

The year I knew there was no Santa Claus was the year he fell asleep beneath the Christmas tree assembling my sister's tricycle.

His favorite pie was something only Grandma Wiggins made: butterscotch custard. Even when my sister and I were kids and loved sweet things, its sweetness made our teeth hurt. I never knew his favorite color. I think he must have had a favorite song, I never knew it, he was always singing, had a song for each occasion, favored "Someone's in the Kitchen with Dinah" while he was washing dishes and "Oh Promise Me" while he was driving in the car. Sometimes, early in the mornings, he'd sing "Buckle Down, Winsocki."

I used to think Winsocki was as funny-sounding a name as that of his favorite politician, Wendell Wilkie. He liked FDR, hated Truman, voted for Dwight Eisenhower. By 1960, I was old enough to reason through my parents' pig Latin and moderately schooled in spelling, so everything they had to say in front of me, they couldn't code. My father was Republican, my mother fell for Kennedy's charisma. "Who did you vote for, John?" my mother asked him that November.

"Mary," my father answered, needing to be secret. "What do you think that curtain in the voting booth is for—?"

"What the hell," he told me later. "If I'd voted like I wanted to, your mother and me, we would have canceled one another out. What's the point of voting like you want to when you know that you'll be canceled out?"

I wonder if he ever dreamed that he could change things. He taught me how to pitch softball. We played croquet in the front yard. He taught me how to spot a plant called preacher-in-the-pulpit along the country roads. He taught me harmony to "Jingle Bells." He taught me how to drive a car. He unscrewed the training wheels and taught me how to ride a bike. He told me strange, portenting things: if I ate too much bread, I'd get dandruff. He read *Reader's Digest, Coronet* and *Pageant* and didn't believe in evolution. There were times I didn't like him. He left abruptly. He left me much unfinished business.

He visited New York City four times in his lifetime. He was in Times Square, a tourist, on V-J Day. Somehow, I'm glad for him, as a believer is for a novitiate, that he was there: celebration needs a crowd. He thought not badly of large cities, after that: but he never lived in one.

He never sailed, his life was landlocked. I think he clammed once, with my uncle, at Virginia Beach. I cannot say for certain that he knew his body's way in water. Water was not an element he knew, except as rain on crops. He was a farmer's son. Without the farmer's land, his legacy was vending farmer's goods. I planted a garden last week, north of where he lived and died, on an island where all roads lead to water. "Now, when you plant a small plot," he once said, "plant what you and yours can eat, or plant what makes you happy, like a sunflower, and offer your surplus to the ones who want. Don't waste. For God's sake, don't waste."

I wish that he could see the things I've sown. Diluted in me is John Wiggins, as today's rain will be in summer's harvest. I wish that I could see him once again, hear his footfalls on the gravel driveway, heavy on one foot: These dried leavings aren't complete in their remembrance, like the trimmings swept from green growth on a grocer's floor, they crumble on my fingertips and fly piecemeal to the wind. I do not do my father justice, that was his charge. I've borne his name, in and out of marriage, a name that is my own, sometimes I wish his strain would leave me, sometimes I'd like to choke it to full bloom. I'd like to turn to him today and say, "I love you: too late: I'm sorry: you did the best you could: you were my father: I learned from you: you were an honest man."

I cultivate a tiny garden, "plot" reminds me of a cemetery. I plant only what my family guarantees to eat. The rest I give to those who want. Had you known him, I'd like to think you would have bought your groceries from John Wiggins. He always had a pleasant word. He could tell you how to plan a meal for twenty people, give you produce wholesale, trim your cut of meat before he weighed it, profit wasn't Daddy's motive, life was. Life defeated him. He taught me how to pack a grocery bag, I worked there weekends, canned goods on the bottom, perishables on top. Someone puts tomatoes on the bottom of my bag these days, I repack it. I was taught respect of certain order. One sees one's father's face, as one grows older, in the most peculiar places. I see Daddy in each bud. I see his stance on corners. I, myself, wear grocer's aprons, when I cook. My mother always said there was no cleaning that damned blood from those white aprons. My father left a stain: I miss him. I write longhand, and in ink.

MARTHA'S VINEYARD
MAY 1979